The Occupant

L.W. Young

CRIMSON CULT MEDIA

Dedicated to Cat 'Choco' Munns, love you bloop.

All rights reserved.

Copyright © 2025 Crimson Cult Media. All rights reserved. Crimson Cult Media supports the right to free expression and the value of copyright. The purpose of copyright is to encourage writers and artists to produce the creative works that enrich our culture. The scanning, uploading, reproduction, transmission in any form or by any means of distribution, electronic or mechanical, including photocopying, recording, or by any information storage or retrieval system of this book without written permission is a theft of the author's intellectual property. If you would like permission to use material from the book (other than for review purposes), please contact crimsoncultmedia@gmail.com. Thank you for your support of the author's rights. For more information please visit https://crimsoncultbooks.com

This book is for entertainment purposes only.

Printed in Oliver Springs, Tennessee, United States of America

Library of Congress Control Number:

Ebook ISBN: 9979-8-89467-039-3

Hardcover ISBN: 9979-8-89467-040-9

Paperback ISBN: 979-8-89467-038-6

Contents

1. Prologue — 1
2. Chapter 1 — 3
3. Chapter 2 — 10
4. Chapter 3 — 16
5. Chapter 4 — 21
6. Chapter 5 — 27
7. Chapter 6 — 34
8. Chapter 7 — 41
9. Chapter 8 — 44
10. Chapter 9 — 48
11. Chapter 10 — 55
12. Chapter 11 — 61
13. Chapter 12 — 67
14. Chapter 13 — 74
15. Chapter 14 — 85
16. Chapter 15 — 92

About the author — 103

1

Prologue

The man waited in the park's bushes and muttered to himself while watching the silent black house across the street. Poppygrow House, 22 St Bernard's Road. Chewing his yellow fingernails and scratching his sores, he knew someone would come by the house soon. The Dark had told him so...

Poppygrow was a detached, two-storey building with buttresses, arched windows, and pointed spires. Nearby was a bus stop, a little corner shop, and the laughter of children could even be heard from a nearby play area. The outside world had done its best to make Poppygrow look like an ordinary house, but even the nearby buildings seemed to pull away from it as it sat gloomily by the main road.

Trying to stay hidden, the man peeked out through the bramble and kept the garish, bloody red front door in his view. The windows were dim, even on this bright summer day, but he knew the layout like the backs of his scaly hands. The 'To Let' sign was gone and it had been almost three weeks since the previous tenant had died, someone *must* be ready to claim that spare room by now.

"Do not fail us," the Dark whispered inside his head.

"I won't," the man spoke aloud to himself, scratching his flaky chin, "have faith in me."

Suddenly, someone came down the road. It was a young lad, with greasy, shoulder length hair trailing out from under his black beanie hat. He was lugging two massive shoulder bags towards the red door, and his white shirt made him pop out against the house's black coating like a dove feather on tar.

"Here he comes," the man muttered excitedly, wetting his lips, "here he comes…"

If things played out well, the man's mental torture from the Dark might soon be coming to an end. Wiping away a tear of relief, the man took note of the house's fresh new lodger as he dumped his bags on the door stop. The young lad didn't know it yet, but everything depended on him now.

There were three sharp knocks, and the man in the bushes shuddered with delight at each sound.

"Do not fail us," the Dark repeated.

"I won't," the man assured once more, "I won't."

2

Chapter 1

When the red door pulled back, Mikey Howes was slightly disappointed to see a short, hefty young woman with a short crop of black hair, wearing a black tank top with fishnet sleeves and fraying grey joggers, and using *way* too much black eyeliner, standing in the doorway.

"Nice to finally meet you Mikey, I'm Everlie," the girl took his hand and beamed upwards at him as if they'd known each other for years, "welcome home!"

Mikey twitched a smile and limply shook her pudgy hands.

"Hey," Mikey obliged, motioning to his bags, "I haven't got much stuff with me, so…"

"No probs, I'll help you," Everlie said, "just let me fetch the agreement papers first."

Everlie left Mikey standing in the doorway with all his Earthly belongings. Mikey checked out the hallway of his new, temporary home. The yellowish wallpaper and minimalist upholstery had faded almost completely to grey. This place probably hadn't been given a lick of paint since the sixties. Down the corridor, past an open broom closet with the nose of a Henry hoover snaking out of it, was a kitchen that looked like it hadn't been cleaned in about as long. Mikey's attention was mostly taken by his new landlady. As the young lady waddled away, Mikey thought her bum looked like two big hams rubbing against each other in those grey joggers. Everlie Bonus, his new landlord's full name, had caught Mikey's attention when he'd seen this property advertised on Zoopla last week. With such a strange surname, Mikey had half wondered (and slightly hoped) that 'Bonus' meant he was getting a little something 'extra' with his tenancy too, perhaps an undercover dominatrix fishing for desperate young men to lock up in her sex dungeon. In that case, the shockingly low rent figure and virtually non-existent admin fee had merely been the icing on the cake.

"Everything okay?" Everlie asked, bouncing back down the creaking stairs with a stack of papers in her hands.

"Oh, sure," Mikey snapped out of his trance, blushing, "I was just thinking about something."

Letting his bags slump to the floor in the dim hallway, Mikey reached out for the tenancy agreement. However, Everlie immediately pulled it away.

"Something wrong?" he looked up, confused, as he grabbed a handful of air.

Everlie was now looking at the floor with her brow clenched.

"Everlie?"

"Listen... there's something I haven't told you about this house yet," Everlie admitted hesitantly, evading his gaze, "Look, could we quickly chat about it in the living room for a minute?"

Mikey shrugged. As far as he was concerned, this place had a roof and central heating, so it went far beyond his needs for the next six months. He had already decided to live with a total stranger, so he doubted there was anything she could say that would scare him off at this point. Probably.

"Sure," he agreed anyway.

Following Everlie through the curtain of shimmering beads, Mikey coughed at the spicy scent from the candles which sat on virtually every flat surface in the living room. The only other lights in the room were from numerous pink and jade crystals lying around. Mikey had no idea why Everlie didn't just open the curtains. There was also an overflowing laundry basket in the corner of the room, as well as numerous half-empty cat bowls filled with pink, puke-looking stuff.

Everlie fell into a wicker rocking chair in the corner, while Mikey lowered himself onto the musky sofa opposite her, happy to be off his blistering feet, as he'd just walked all the way from the town's youth hostel.

"Watch out for the cat!" Everlie warned before Mikey dropped onto the chair.

"Oh, shit," Mikey shot back up, barely avoiding the furball whose grey coat matched perfectly with the lumpy, fuzzy sofa.

Dozily, the cat looked up at Mikey, unimpressed.

"That's Wicca," Everlie giggled, "*she* owns this place really."

"Right," Mikey nodded as he perched himself on the opposite side, Wicca giving him one last disapproving stare before going back to sleep.

"Listen, about the room, there's something I didn't say on the Zoopla page," Everlie sighed, "or even in our emails."

"Oh?" Mikey nodded, half paying attention.

Everlie took a deep breath, and fished out a silver, heart shaped locket from down the front of her top. She rubbed it fiercely as she spoke to him.

"So, the thing is, you can't change anything in your room for the time being," Everlie blurted, "for the first month or so, the posters, decorations, and bed sheets all have to stay exactly as they are, okay?"

"Okay," Mikey shrugged, wiping his nose, "fine by me."

"Sentimental value," Everlie elaborated, looking him in the eyes, "it's a 'me' thing, and it won't have to be forever, it's just... important to me for now, okay?"

"It's fine," Mikey chuckled, looking around, "don't worry about it."

"And there's also one other thing."

Across from him, Everlie was wringing her fingerless black gloves, and her shoulders were trembling. Mikey started to shift uncomfortably in his seat. What was *with* this girl?

"Oh yeah?" He gave a cursory smile.

'Sex dungeon. Sex dungeon. Sex dungeon!'

'Shut up,' he silently scolded himself.

Looking at the ground, Everlie clasped her fidgeting hands in her lap.

"Okay, so here's the thing, between the hours of two and three in the morning, you can't leave your room," Everlie announced, "not under any circumstances, okay?"

Mikey just sat in silence. Finally, he twitched a nervous laugh.

"*Any* circumstances?" he asked with a lopsided grin.

Everlie shook her head.

"No matter what you hear outside," she told him seriously, "you must remain *inside* the room during those hours. Got it?"

Mikey was quiet for a minute and then just laughed.

"You're joking," he grinned confidently, wondering if they were already on teasing terms yet (it had taken about four weeks to get to that point with Amy).

"I'm not."

Everlie's stony eyes told him everything he needed to know. She was dead serious. Mikey let out a long, shaky sigh.

"You're right," Mikey sat up with a whistle, scratching his neck, "that *is* a weird one."

Mikey found himself looking at Wicca as if *she* might have an answer for what to say next, but the cat remained curled up silently.

"But, let's say, what if..." Mikey hesitated, still unsure if Everlie was being serious, "what if I need the toilet?"

"Then I'm afraid you'll have to hold it in," Everlie nodded.

"But what if there's a fire?"

"Don't worry," Everlie assured, "there won't be anything like that. Trust me."

Mikey just stared at her, twitching an unsure smile. This *had* to be a joke.

"I mean... why didn't you tell me about this earlier?" Mikey asked, his eyes going to the door, "it's not like there weren't plenty of opportunities, we were emailing each other for weeks."

Everlie forced herself to look at him, biting her bottom lip, and wringing her hands again.

"Truthfully, I was worried that it'd scare you off," Everlie sighed, squeezing her knees together.

"I can understand," Mikey tried to sound sympathetic, "but..."

Everlie's gaze went to the darkened window, covered by a cotton drape, and stared listlessly out of it.

"I know it's an unusual request but, I..." she hung her head, "I *need* this rent money Mikey, otherwise I can't keep living here."

"Look, it's fine," Mikey told her, "But at least tell me why I can't leave the room, okay?"

Everlie released a quick, deep breath like an Olympian diver getting ready to take a medal winning jump.

"During those hours, I need privacy... privacy for something I'm working on. A personal project," Everlie explained in a hurry, "it's difficult to explain, but I can't be distracted while I'm working on it, okay?"

Everlie closed her eyes and tried to compose herself. Mikey just continued to sit squashed at the end of the sofa with his legs pressed together so as to not to disturb the sleeping animal beside him. This was weird, *very* weird, and he didn't know what he was supposed to do or say next. Across from him, Everlie became glum.

"Night owl, huh?" was all he could say.

"So, do you still want to sign this agreement or not?" she shrugged, flapping the papers at him, "it's fine if you don't anymore."

Mikey didn't know what to say. From her eyes alone, he could tell it *wasn't* fine.

"Uh..."

"Look, it's fine if you want to reconsider, really," Everlie now looked away, wiping her eyes, and shrugging despondently, "you wouldn't be the first person to turn me down."

"Wait."

As he said it, a gasp got caught in Everlie's throat, and she looked at him with such cow eyed sadness that Mikey honestly thought his heart might break. The truth was that Mikey needed to get away from his old life as quickly as possible, and Poppygrow House was the fastest way to achieve this, weird landlady or not.

"I suppose..." he sighed a big, defeated breath, "I suppose I wasn't planning on doing much at 2am anyway."

A toothy smile lit up Everlie's face. Mikey smiled back, while a dark corner of his mind told him that he was just being a Simp.

'I honestly don't care,' he told himself, 'I need a new life, and I need it now.'

"Yes!" she squealed while rocking on the chair, clenching her fists to the sky in delight, "thank you Mikey, THANK YOU!

"It's okay," Mikey chuckled, a little taken aback, "chill."

"God bless you, Mikey," Everlie collected herself, wiping a small tear from her black rimmed eyelash, "you honestly don't know how much this means to me."

Mikey smiled softly at her as he patted himself down for a pen (despite knowing he didn't have one).

"Oh, let me get one for you!" Everlie shot up eagerly and darted across the room.

Mikey saluted her with a gesture of thanks as his eyes followed her out. Turning his head to the front door, Mikey caught a glimpse into the hallway and noticed that he hadn't shut the front door behind him on the way in (Amy had always scolded him for that). Staring past the red front door into the open air, Mikey now noticed something, a figure standing across the road. He was dressed in a heavy blue macintosh, even in the blazing hot sun, and was standing dead still with his arms by his sides. Mikey leaned forward, trying to pick out the details of this bearded fellow's wasted face and agape mouth. In the sun, the figure's wide eyes glistened like white marbles, staring right at Mikey...

"Here's one!"

Mikey hadn't heard Everlie barrelling back down the old staircase with a fountain pen in her hand, slamming the front door closed with her backside as she returned to the living room.

Mikey, returning to reality, scribbled his signature on the contract.

Chapter 2

After dragging his bags up the rickety staircase and shouldering through his new bedroom door (it took a few hard shoves), Mikey fell inside and was immediately blinded by the garish pink walls. After the gloom of the rest of the house, being in here was like seeing a rainbow at a funeral.

"Fuck me," he muttered, dropping his bags, "I guess Barbie went back to her Dream House then?"

The bed frame had a love heart engraved on the headboard, and the baby-blue star dotted bed sheets were just about tolerable. However, the monster Taylor Swift poster taking up half the far wall just *had* to go. Mikey stamped over to take it down but suddenly felt a hard rumbling in his pocket. He checked his phone.

It was Amy.

"Oh shit," he sighed, looking around for help.

All Taylor could offer was a mean glare over her diamond encrusted microphone with pouty eyes that suggested he was one of the good-for-nothing ex-boyfriends she was currently singing about.

The phone buzzed again.

'*Maybe she's calling to apologise?*'

The stray thought was enough for Mikey to accept the call.

"Hello?" he answered sulkily.

"Mikey? Thank *God!*" Amy sighed, "I've been trying to reach you for days!"

"Sorry," Mikey evaded, shutting the curtains, and dampening the sun's light into a burning red hue, "been busy."

"Right, sorry," Amy hesitated, "well… how's it going?"

Mikey paused. Was she really asking that?

"I've been better, honestly," Mikey laughed, crossing the room, and shoving the door closed.

"Sorry, stupid question," Amy sighed, "listen, Mikey, I'm calling to say that I… I feel bad about what happened between us, okay?"

"Me too."

"Look, I'll cut to the chase," she told him, "I'm an open door, okay?"

More silence. This duel was getting complicated.

'An open door?' Mikey thought, 'what the heck is that supposed to mean?'

"It's a bit late for that now."

"Look, Mikey, don't be…"

'Childish?' Mikey wanted to cut in, 'isn't *that* what you called me last time?'

"No, I mean, it's *literally* too late for that," he said instead, wiping his brow, "I've found a new place."

"A new place?" Amy asked, "what do you mean?"

"I mean, I've moved in with someone else," Mikey explained in a hurry, "I literally just signed the tenancy agreement a few minutes ago…"

"You've…" Amy gasped, "you've WHAT!?"

"Look, don't freak out," Mikey cupped the speaker, lowering his voice.

"Seriously?" Amy stuttered, "w... why are you doing this to me?"

"What do you mean 'why'?" he lowered his voice, "we broke up, didn't we?"

"I mean, well... I guess," Amy collected herself, "but... how did you find somewhere so quickly?"

"I got lucky, I suppose," Mikey went to the curtains and peeked out, just to check that creepy mac-wearing dude wasn't still hanging around, "I'm out of your hair now, aren't I?"

"I... but why didn't you tell me!?"

"The owner needed someone immediately," Mikey was getting impatient now.

"But Mikey, you were gone only a few weeks ago!" Mikey knew Amy had her eyes closed and was massaging her brow like she *always* did during these arguments, "all your stuff is here!"

"Keep it!" Mikey cut her off, "I can't keep doing this Amy."

"I... Mikey, I've *told* you what I want," Amy sounded on the edge of tears now, "I just want an apology, that's all."

Mikey shuddered, closing his eyes.

"Mikey?" Amy asked, sounding concerned, "are you still there?"

Mikey hung up the phone.

He just could not face going over the same talking points again. Slapping the phone on the desk, Mikey jammed his hands in his pockets and stared at the red-lit floor, digging his toes into it. Why should he apologise? There were *tons* of boyfriends out there who did much shittier things than what he had done. Crazy bitch.

The word made Mikey's thoughts stop in their tracks. Bitch. This was the word he was using to describe the woman who'd once called him her "true sweetheart" while clutching his hand walking through York's cobblestone streets on their 3rd date anniversary, the same woman who made the most delicious egg fried rice every Thursday when he came home from work. In the year of our lord, August 13th, 2022, Mikey Howes now thought his "cheeky sausage" ex-girlfriend Amy Russell was a crazy bitch.

Standing alone in some stranger's pink bedroom while their teddy bears watched him from atop a wardrobe, Mikey started to tear up. He instantly hated himself for it.

"Snap out of it," he gritted his teeth and slapped his own cheek, "don't be a pussy, yeah?"

Looking up, he once again caught sight of Taylor Swift looking over the lip of her microphone, glaring at him like he was the biggest shit-lord on the planet.

"Oh yeah? Well, fuck you too, Swifty," Mikey grumbled as he ripped the poster down.

Turning back to the curtains, Mikey threw them open again and purposefully planted his hands on his hips as the sun warmed him through the large, single glazed window overlooking the messy garden. No matter what came before, there would be changes around here alright. From this day forward, Mikey Howes was starting again.

However, first he needed to cheer himself up, which called for some porn watching.

Leaving his room and re-entering the musky gloom of the rest of the house, Mikey tiptoed across the landing and gently tapped on Everlie's closed door.

"Everlie?" he asked softly.

No answer.

"Are you busy?" Mikey approached again.

Before his knuckles reached the door, it pulled back so fast that it made Mikey jump. Everlie's big face filled his vision.

"What is it?" she snapped at him, "I was working on something!"

Mikey did a double take, this was not the same bouncy, bubbly goth girl he'd been chatting to moments earlier. Behind her, all Mikey could see of Everlie's darkened bedroom were a few pale spots of light, and candles which barely illuminated the hanging Evanescence poster on the far wall. The smell of incense made Mikey feel lightheaded; how much of that stuff was she going through each day?

"Sorry," Everlie walked back with her head in her hands, "sorry I spoke to you like that."

"It's fine, I guess," he winced, "A... Are you okay?"

"Yeah, fine, I was just... it doesn't matter," Everlie sighed, scratching her brow, "anyway, what do you want?"

"Right, sorry," Mikey cleared his throat, "I was just wondering if I could nab the Wi-Fi code from you?"

"Oh, right," Everlie realised, nodding, "sorry, this house doesn't have internet."

It took Mikey a few seconds to process what she'd just said.

"What?" Mikey gasped, "you're joking!"

"Afraid not, having access to it was bad for our... for my mental health," Everlie shrugged, "I've been going to the local library to send emails and such."

Mikey tried to imagine what kind of person in 2022 would not have access to an internet connection. Even with her quirks, Everlie still didn't seem to fit the bill.

"I see," Mikey stumbled, not wanting to sound rude, "but... your old housemate used it, right?"

"We never needed it," Everlie's face became stony, her eyes glazing over, "we had each other..."

Looking at her, Mikey suddenly found he wanted to change the topic as quickly as possible.

"Well, I still need to use it," Mikey began, mentally exhausted by the idea of coping without YouTube for an evening, "what am *I* going to do?"

"Tell you what, I'll order you one to come soonish," Everlie explained like an impatient parent, "that okay?"

"I..." Mikey rolled his eyes, "I suppose it's better than nothing."

"Okay," Everlie offered him a sickly-sweet smile before slinking back into her room, "ta."

Before Mikey could say anything else, she'd closed the door and left him standing on the landing. Whatever she was doing in her room, she was keen to get back to it.

"Fair fair," Mikey said to no one in particular, slinking back to his own room.

Having Internet from next week would be better than nothing, but it didn't exactly help him tonight. Also, he had a horrible feeling that the drive with all his porn on it was still at Amy's place. Hopefully she hadn't thrown it out.

Going back to his room, Mikey decided that he'd put his headphones on and watch his personal collection of pirated 00's TV shows until he drifted to sleep...

Chapter 3

Mikey woke up in complete darkness.

Sitting up in a hurry, he pulled his headphones out. Where was he? Where was Amy? Why were there weird looking teddy bears on top of the dresser by the door?

'Oh yeah,' he remembered sleepily, wiping his eyes.

Pulling himself upright on his new bed, which had been surprisingly comfy, Mikey collected his bearings. He'd fallen asleep in his clothes. The light of the pale moon turned the pink walls around him into a cold shade of blue. His two luggage bags were sitting on the wood slatted floor. At his feet, the media player on his laptop was halfway through his playlist of *The Sopranos*.

Mikey rubbed his tired eyes and put his feet on the ground. In his half-awake state, Mikey knew one only thing: he was absolutely bursting for a piss.

Standing upright, Mikey floated like a drunkard towards the door, taking a big stride over his unpacked luggage bags with only one thing on his mind: toilet. However, before Mikey could reach out for the metal handle, a pressing thought struck him.

'What time is it?'

Everlie had told him not to leave the room between two and three in the morning, he wasn't going to forget that weird conversation in a hurry. Going back to the laptop, Mikey squinted at the clock in the corner of his desktop. 2:05.

"Shit," he muttered.

Everlie's request rang in his mind.

'You'll have to hold it in...'

Fuck that.

Mikey went back to the door, sifting through the list of excuses he'd use if Everlie caught him. It was only five minutes past the hour, so Mikey figured there'd be plenty of time for Everlie to do her 'personal project', whatever it was (probably rubbing one out to Ronnie Radke or something).

Mikey pulled the metal handle to his bedroom door, but it was stuck.

"Huh?" Mikey tried again.

The door wouldn't even give an inch.

As his eyes adjusted to the darkness, Mikey now noticed there was a locking device under the handle. Becoming more awake, in no small part due to the pressure on his bladder, Mikey ran his fingers along it and discovered a keyhole. Had Everlie locked him in? Mikey reeled, shocked. Was this really happening? Everlie had told him not to leave the room, sure, but locking him in was a step too far!

Mikey tried the handle again, shaking and heaving, but achieved nothing.

"This isn't right, Everlie!" Mikey now banged on the door, losing his patience, "open up!"

No answer.

Mikey's heart raced. He scanned the room. The door was a big old hunk of thick wood with its hinges on the outside, no *way* could he kick it down even if he wanted to. Searching helplessly, the mouthless face of the bears sitting on top of the drawers seemed to taunt him.

'Don't be scared, Mikey-boy, mindlessly throwing yourself into a housing situation like this always *works in your favour, doesn't it?'* Mikey imagined the bear goading him as he felt his way along the wall for the light switch, *'I'm sure things will turn out fine, they always do for you...'*

"Shut up, dickhead," Mikey put his hands over his ears, immediately embarrassed that he was actually arguing with a stuffed animal.

But the bear made some good points. What if Everlie *never* let him out of here?

"That's just my bladder talking," Mikey assured himself, trying to regain composure, "I'll get out of here soon, I just need to stay calm..."

Then, Mikey noticed something: there was a faint glow flickering from beneath his locked door. The effect of the rippling, pale shadow was unmistakable. There was also the burning smell of incense, and flickers of smoke rising from beneath the gap from the floor. Someone was burning candles out there. Mikey put his ear against the door.

"Everlie?" Mikey knocked, softer this time, "are you out there?"

No response.

"Everlie?"

Silence.

No, that wasn't totally true, Mikey could hear something. He put his ear to the door, momentarily forgetting the reason why he'd wanted to leave the room in the first place. It was a human noise, a murmur that rose and fell in quick succession between gasps of breath.

Was Everlie talking to someone outside his room?

Mikey's face became very hot, and his breath turned rapid and shallow. The nightmare scenario he'd jokingly told himself earlier had suddenly become true; this goth chick was a bloody *Witch*.

'Please let this be a dream,' he thought, clenching his eyes shut, *'this has to be a dream...'*

But the noise was becoming clearer, and these breathy gasps were not muttering, but weeping.

"Everlie?" Mikey wrapped his knuckles gently on the door, lowering his voice to a hush, "are you okay?"

No answer, but the weeping continued. The sound was wet and strained, punctuated by exhausted shudders and sharp intakes of breath. It was almost as if the person making these noises was doing all they could to keep tears at bay. And these noises weren't coming from outside his room...

They were coming from within it.

A sliver of ice fell down his spine. Mikey turned but saw no one there. However, the weeping remained. Licking his dry lips, his breath quickening, Mikey strained his ears until he could pinpoint the source of the muffled sound. It was coming from under his bed. The only thing separating Mikey and the hiding, crying figure, was the hanging duvet Mikey had knocked down with his feet on his way to the door.

"H... hey?" Mikey asked the air, "is someone there?"

No response. The crying continued. Tiptoeing across the room, Mikey held out a shaking hand towards the bed.

"STAY AWAY!"

The shrill command stopped Mikey in his tracks, and he almost pissed himself. The female voice was full of raw pain, and Mikey swore he could pinpoint the shuffling of bare skin and nails against the wooden floorboards. Whoever was under there was clawing to push themselves against the wall. The weeping continued, but the figure remained hidden by the hanging duvet. Trembling in the cold night air, Mikey felt obliged to stay as far away as possible. That was until...

"Don't you understand?" the voice under the bed shrieked, "I can't be with you now, and NOT EVER AGAIN!"

Mikey's heart leapt in his chest.

"Amy?" he almost screamed.

Without thinking, Mikey raced to the side of the bed and pulled back the duvet...

*

...And instantly woke up the next morning.

The fresh lemon glare of the sun hurt his eyes as he rubbed his face. There was a puddle soaking his crotch.

"Urgh," he moaned, knowing exactly what it was.

But for some reason, Mikey hadn't woken up in bed. He'd woken up exactly where he'd been standing in his dream.

CHAPTER 4

"Oh dear, had a little accident, eh?"

Mikey had been trying to get his bundle of piss-soaked clothes to the washing machine without his housemate noticing, but Everlie's bedroom door had been open when he'd left his room. The weary, snarky comment she'd greeted him with from her bed sounded too tired to be wholly mean-spirited. Truthfully, she sounded exhausted.

"I'm just putting a wash on," Mikey blushed, tiptoeing down the spiral staircase towards the kitchen.

After chucking his wet clothes (and shoes, which had also been soaked) into the washing machine, Mikey went back up to his bedroom where Everlie met him in the doorway holding a sponge and a bottle of Dettol.

"I should clean it up," Mikey laughed nervously, trying to squeeze past her into the room, "it's no problem, honest."

Usually when he said something like this to Amy when delegating housework, it was a sure-fire way of getting her to do it while also ridding him of the guilt.

"It's fine," Everlie sighed as she went to her knees and kept scrubbing.

Mikey remained in the doorway, staring down helplessly at Everlie mopping up. However, Everlie suddenly stopped, her head slanted curiously.

"Something wrong?" Mikey asked.

"Maddy's Taylor Swift poster" Everlie pointed to the empty spot on the wall, "where's it gone?"

Mikey's heart caught in his throat as he looked over to where he'd dumped the fallen poster pieces in the corner of the room. Sheepishly, Mikey offered her an apologetic smile before she hurried over to investigate. Wielding the two torn pieces of the once fabulous pop star, Everlie shook them at him, looking angrier than she'd been about the literal piss on the floor.

"Seriously Mikey?" she scowled, "I told you not to touch anything in here!"

Mikey just waved his arms in a limp apology. Standing on tiptoes, Everlie made a strained attempt to attach the poster back to the baby pink wallpaper using the Blu Tack residue, but her stumpy arms couldn't reach. Grunting, she threw the pieces on the floor. Mikey flinched. Not looking at him, Everlie put her hands on her hips and shook her head, muttering something like "...no wonder I had poor results last night," which Mikey overheard.

"I'm sorry?" he inquired, stepping forward.

"I *did* give you very clear instructions," Everlie cut him off, "it's really important that you don't move any of Maddy's things, understand?"

"Sorry," Mikey rubbed the nape of his neck bashfully, "are you expecting her to come back then?"

Mikey felt his face go flush red. He'd just relapsed into the same passive aggressive tone which had gotten him into so much trouble with Amy over the years. Everlie however, simply turned her eyes to the floor.

"It's complicated," she muttered vacantly, "anyway, just let me sort this out now, okay?"

Before Mikey could say anything else, Everlie had closed the door in front of him.

"H... hey!" Mikey reeled as the wood stopped inches from his face, shutting him out of his own room.

No response. Shrugging, Mikey left her to it, with not the energy for a second argument with a crazy young woman in as many days. Retreating to the downstairs living room to play games on his phone, Wicca offered no sympathy from her usual spot, kneading the grey sofa cushion with her rough claws. Listening to the scraping and banging from his room upstairs, Mikey got the feeling Everlie was doing far more than just cleaning the floor up there. Whatever, as long as she didn't touch his stuff. Mikey turned to the window, it was another sunny one, but the heat inside the dark living room only made him feel stuffy and tense. He ran his longish hair through his fingers as he hunched over on the couch. Was this *really* what he'd had in mind when he'd imagined 'getting away' from his old life?

'If it stinks everywhere you go, maybe you're *the one who needs a shower.'*

That had been one of Amy's sayings.

"No," Mikey decided as he sat up, tapping his foot, "it's not just me this time."

Be that as it may, he'd signed the contract, so he couldn't just pack up and leave this place now, could he?

'I can in six months when the contract's up,' he thought with a newfound resolve as we went to get his shoes from the laundry drying rack, 'right now, I just need some fresh air.'

A break would do him good, a little wander around town to clear his head perhaps? After that, he might come back with a new sense of appreciation for this living situation, unconventional as it was. In a weird way, it reminded him of being a student again.

"I'm going out!" Mikey called up the stairs with one hand on the front door handle, "might go to a pub or something this evening, okay?"

Mikey didn't hear a reply, just the sound of Everlie working and rearranging stuff in his room.

Shaking his head, Mikey stepped out into the summer afternoon sunshine. He stuffed his hands in his jean pockets and let the door slam behind him, walking towards the city centre. As Mikey escaped the charcoal shadow of Poppygrow House, he felt the sun peek through the sparse cloud cover and warm his face. He might call Brian later and ask him out for a drink, another pleasant distraction to get his mind off things (or at least drunk enough to not notice them for a while).

Up the road ahead, Mikey could see something blocking his path. Shielding his eyes, he tried to get a better look. There was a man standing there, an unmoving shadow with a wasted face and wearing a dark blue macintosh. Almost tripping over his feet, Mikey recognised him as the same strange, skeletal man who had been staring at him from across the street on the day he'd moved in.

Once again, the man appeared to be sweltering in his faded mac, which was even more haggard up close. The man's thin skin pressed against his bones, turning his head into something like a skull. Below the waistline of his coat, which went down to his knees, the man's bony legs seemed to be completely bare. His eyes stared with hollow intent, as if he were looking right through Mikey. Mikey shuddered and hugged himself, the air around him suddenly feeling very cold indeed.

"Alright, mate," Mikey saluted as he walked around the unmoving man, stepping off the curb and into the road.

The man's eyes followed him. Mikey increased his pace.

"You've heard her…" the elderly man's rusty voice made Mikey flinch, "haven't you?"

Mikey was turning to check that the old man had been talking to him, when something grabbed his arm.

"Ow!" Mikey now spun around, "what the…"

Mikey found himself locking eyes with the old man, who was now close enough for Mikey to read every crack on his face and taste the rot of his breath.

"Get off me!" Mikey demanded as animal fear took over.

Pulling frantically, Mikey tried to get out of the man's grasp, but those bony fingers held him tight. How could such a frail old man have such strength? Then, the old man leaned towards Mikey, his eyes more intense than ever.

"You've heard her, haven't you?" he uttered, "Free yourself, before it's too late!"

"I…" Mikey trembled, "I…"

Then, suddenly, the old man lunged forward with his mouth open wide, trying to bite him.

"FUCK OFF!"

Mikey's primal responses kicked into gear. Twisting his arm, Mikey slipped his exposed fingers out from the old man's rotting teeth and gave him an almighty shove with his other arm. The old geezer's foot caught the edge of the curb, sending him toppling over into the road.

Mikey just stood red faced, huffing, and puffing, while the mac-wearing scarecrow lay sprawled in the road, eyes rolling backwards and breath heaving as if in some state of exasperated euphoria.

"Oi!"

Mikey spun towards the new voice. Across the street, an overweight man walking his dog had spotted the scuffle and was pointing squarely at Mikey. The dog joined in, yapping, and pulling its leash towards the nasty young man who had just pushed over the nice old, mac-clad cannibal. In the corner of his eye, Mikey could see the geezer he'd shoved into the road starting to get up again.

Mikey ran for it, and the dog's yapping seemed to follow him all the way to the pub.

CHAPTER 5

"Cheer up matey," Brian slapped Mikey's back, "you look like you're hiding from something."

Mikey twitched a smile and hunched over his pint protectively. The pub was rowdy with clashing voices, chinking glasses, and the steady thump of modern mumble-rap (the appeal of which totally confused Mikey, he'd rather be listening to something like 'Mr. Brightside' or 'Sex on Fire' like this dive used to play). Watching over his shoulder, Mikey sank further into his seat as he observed how much younger everyone in here looked than him.

"Maybe I am," Mikey answered eventually.

"Relax," Brian leaned back on his stool, "I doubt you're going to run into Amy here."

Mikey rolled his eyes and necked the last of his pint. All he'd wanted to do was keep his head down, drown his sorrows, and have a nice distracting evening, but Brian kept on reminding him of everything. Mikey looked up at him. Across the table, his friend kept that smug knowing grin on his face, even Brian's sweating pint of Diet Coke seemed to taunt him.

"I'm not worried about that," Mikey grumbled, wiping his lips, "I've got nothing left to say to her anyway."

"Shame," Brian shrugged, circling his finger around the rim of his glass, "I liked her."

Mikey found the music in here was really starting to give him a headache, he'd probably need another beer soon.

"Still," Brian lifted his head, "sounds like you've got a new squeeze now and all."

Mikey almost spat his drink out.

"Everlie's not my squeeze mate," Mikey coughed, wiping his lips, "she's my bloody landlady!"

"Oh yeah?" Brian raised his eyebrows, "even with all that weird shit she's making you do at night?"

"Occupational hazards mate. Besides, it's worth it for the money I'm saving," Mikey looked away, "do you know how difficult it is finding a cheap place in this economy?"

"Fair enough," Brian accepted, "still, bit keen innit?"

By 'keen', Mikey knew Brian meant 'desperate'. Or 'rushed'. Or 'stupid'. In any case, these words could all describe Mikey's current situation. The truth certainly hurt.

"I... I just needed to get away from Amy, okay?" Mikey's brow furrowed like he was focussing on a very difficult question, "I didn't have many options."

"Suppose you could have stayed with Steph and I for a bit?" Brian suggested.

"Nah, I wouldn't want to be a third wheel for you guys," Mikey laughed with a note of embarrassment, "besides, neither of you would want me there right now."

"Honestly, I'd be okay with it," Brian scoffed, taking another sip of his coke, "Steph on the other hand..."

"I'm staying at Poppygrow House on St. Bernard's Street," Mikey changed the topic, not wanting to hear about yet *another* woman who hated him, "maybe you guys could come visit sometime. Everlie's a bit weird, but..."

Mikey was cut off by the sound of Brian choking on his drink. Mikey patiently held up his hand, so he wasn't instantly covered in a shower of cola.

"St. *Bernard's*?!" Brian's spluttered, "Christ mate, no wonder your rent's so cheap then."

Mikey leant back in his seat, narrowing his gaze.

"What do you mean?"

"You should be careful around that neck of the woods, my man," Brian leant over the table, his eyes cold and serious, "someone got stabbed up there."

"Stabbed?" Mikey's grip tightened around his glass, "Who? When?"

"It was some poor girl, about a month ago," Brian shook his head, "police say they found her with, get this, *bite* marks all over her. So weird. Steph would have a field day over it, she *loves* true crime stuff."

"Bite... marks?" Mikey trembled, not fully hearing him.

Brian replied with something else, but Mikey didn't really hear that either. The rabble of the pub seemed to fade around him, and painful memories flashed in Mikey's mind.

"Mikey," Brian now leaned across the table, "are you okay?"

Mikey was sweating, and his heartbeat was pulsing in his ears. Mikey could usually cope with morbid stories, but this instance had triggered something in him. Was it just because of the old man who'd attacked him earlier?

'You've heard her, haven't you... HAVEN'T YOU!?'

No, it was something else. Something alarmingly familiar...

"I... need to go to the bathroom," Mikey uttered, suddenly feeling sick.

As he got up, the table lurched, and he almost found himself going over the top of it. Mikey hadn't noticed he'd been on his fifth pint until he stood up and the room started spinning.

"Whoa, careful mate," Brian came up alongside him to offer support.

"Git' off!"

Clumsily, Mikey swatted Brian's arm away, side-eying him as he finished the last droplets of his drink and dropped the empty glass back on the table. This 'friend' of his had been ribbing him all night about losing Amy and was now trying to tease him with ridiculous stories about stabbings and local cannibals. Pathetic.

"Mikey," Brian said with a hurt laugh, "we cool?"

Mikey didn't answer as he made for the bathroom, putting his hands on the walls for support. The floor swayed as he left Brian's table. Someone must have turned the music up because it was now the only thing Mikey could hear over the thumping of his own heart. Trying to catch his bearings, he swayed backwards and looked for the toilet door.

Then, looking up, Mikey saw him.

Mikey froze. Standing across the room near where the windows overlooked the pub garden was a skull-faced old man in a faded mac, still staring with those intense beady eyes. Leaning against the wall, Mikey rubbed his stinging eyes to check he wasn't hallucinating. He wasn't. That nutter had followed him here.

Mikey gulped, instantly becoming sober, as his eyes flitted from left to right. No one else in the pub seemed to notice the presence of this gaunt, pale horror interloping among the normal people. The spectre began floating past the tables in a beeline towards Mikey. For a while, Mikey forgot that he'd needed the toilet and could almost taste the man's rotting breath. The man's lips were moving, shuddering. Mikey knew what the man was saying without even needing to hear it.

"You've heard her, haven't you?" those lips mouthed, "You've heard her, haven't you?"

'Move!'

Reality finally caught up with Mikey's beer-addled brain, and he stumbled back in the direction of the pub entrance, ignoring Brian's attempt to flag him down.

But then, someone grabbed his arm.

Panting, Mikey spun around to face the person now pinning him against the wall. It was Everlie, her moon face eclipsing everything else. Throttling his wrist, Everlie stared daggers at him through her drooping fringe of raven black hair.

"Here you are!" she seethed, teeth clenched, "lose track of time, did you?!"

"Wha…" Mikey could only manage, barely comprehending what was going on.

Everlie dragged him away. With hardly any strength in his legs, Mikey had no choice but to comply. Like a helpless dog, Mikey was led across the bar floor.

"E… Everlie?" Mikey slurred, his mind catching up with the reality of 20 seconds ago, "what are you doing here?"

"It's almost midnight!" she bellowed, not even looking at him.

"What?" Mikey could only respond, "why is that important?"

Everlie refused to elaborate as she ploughed through the idlers and chatters on the bar floor with one arm out for guidance. Mikey checked over his shoulder for the gaunt old spectre again but couldn't see him now.

"Is this your new Mistress then?" Brian doffed an imaginary cap to the pair as they straggled past him.

"Piss off Brian!" Mikey groaned before being pushed through the exit and thrown into the cold.

As the music ducked out, Mikey's trainers skidded across the cobblestone street, and a cool blast of night air splashed over him.

"What's your problem?" Mikey spun to Everlie, hugging his bare, goose-pimply arms.

Everlie just stood there, panting, and heaving like she was ready to punch him. Her round face was a contorting mixture of stress, anger, and genuine unhappiness.

"It's. Getting. Late!" she jabbed a pudgy, sausage finger at him with each word.

"So?" Mikey shivered.

"What do you mean, 'so'?" she bellowed, "you must be *in* your room at 2am, okay?"

Mikey's jaw hung slack in disbelief.

"Didn't I make myself clear!?" she screamed.

"Yes, but..."

Ignoring him, Everlie swung her finger around until she was pointing at a beat up, red Honda sitting on the curb outside with smoke still billowing out of the exhaust, the same car Mikey had seen sitting in Everlie's driveway when he'd arrived yesterday.

"You're coming back home with me now," she shouted, "or you'll need a new place to live from next month, got it?"

The commotion drew a few raised eyebrows from the onlookers milling around outside. No options left; Mikey fell through the open passenger seat door of the Honda. Too drunk, confused, and embarrassed to argue with Everlie further, Mikey's knees came right up to his chin as he nestled himself into the cramped shotgun seat. Everlie made the whole car bounce as she plummeted into the driver's side and stabbed her key in the ignition. Mikey could do nothing but sit in silence, now a lowly prisoner.

As they drove away, Mikey's fingers pawed the passenger window. The sanctuary of the pub drifted out of view, but Mikey had been half hoping to spot Brian come running out after him, maybe to give Mikey one last chance to mouth 'sorry' for dragging his mate out for such a bummer of an evening. Instead, Mikey only saw the gaunt, mac-wearing spectre, staring after the departing car. Mikey's heart lurched in his chest at the sight of him. There was something distinctly different about the man this time than their previous encounters.

Watching the car leaving, the old man had been smiling.

Chapter 6

The car arrived in the driveway of Poppygrow House at just after one in the morning. Parking up, Everlie killed the engine and braced herself against the steering wheel. The interior lights went out. In the passenger seat, Mikey glared at her through the darkness. Outside, it was starting to rain.

"Right," Everlie then sighed, whipping the key from the ignition, "in we go."

"No."

Everlie's black coated lips pressed into a tight line as Mikey stared back at her, gripping her wrist.

"I'm not going back in that house until you tell me what's really going on," he said.

"Or what?" she scoffed, looking away, "you'll leave?"

"That's right," Mikey declared calmly.

Everlie released a gasp of terror.

"I'm ripping up our contract, taking my bags, and leaving first thing tomorrow morning," Mikey went on, "That is, unless you come clean."

Everlie shook him off, slamming her face down into her palms.

"What exactly is this 'personal project' of yours?" he leaned forward, "Why are you doing it so late at night? Why do you need *me*?"

"I... There *is* no 'personal project', okay?" she cried, wiping her eyes, "I made it all up."

"Why?" Mikey pressed her, "tell me what's really going on here!"

Shutting her eyes, Everlie put her neck against the headrest and released a long, heavy breath.

"There *is* an explanation for all of this, I promise," she whispered, "I didn't tell you everything before, but... but please hear me out, okay?"

Mikey sat back, listening intently. Everlie wiped the smudging mascara from her face as she spoke.

"The girl who used to live in your room, Maddy, is... was... my best friend since childhood. We lived together for many years," Everlie released, "when my parents abandoned me in my late teens, she was there for me. We both took dual ownership of Poppygrow House, the house I was born in."

Everlie tilted her head in the direction of the dark building. Mikey glanced through the window, and Poppygrow House silently agreed. Everlie looked at the dark building, a smile rising on her tear-stained face.

"So, you and Maddy... lived together?" Mike butted in softly, "what happened?"

"Last month, we... We had a big fight," Everlie grimaced, head bowed, "She ran out of the house. I never saw her again."

A sudden, wrenching sob erupted from Everlie's throat. Mikey nodded with grave understanding, and remembered what Brian had told him at the pub.

"I heard someone got stabbed up there... covered in bite marks".

"I'm so sorry Everlie, I had no idea," Mikey approached softly, "but what does this all have to do with me?"

Everlie pushed back into her seat, gripping the wheel again.

"The police say that Maddy was killed between two and three o'clock in the morning," Everlie confessed with her eyes clenched shut, "And since then, every night, I... I think I can hear her voice coming from that room. Calling me."

Mikey sat upright.

"C... Calling you?"

Everlie tittered; the sound weighed down with bitter sadness.

"Crazy, right?" she now gazed up towards Mikey's window, "but I hear it every night. Every. Single. Night."

Mikey gulped and said nothing. Mikey could still recall the desperate, clawing scream from his dream.

"STAY AWAY!"

Everlie sounded far less crazy than he'd have liked her to.

"Therefore, I need someone to be in that room during those hours," Everlie sniffed, her shaking arms gripping the wheel, "if I follow that voice, I... I think I'll finally go mad."

"Why not just lock the door?" Mikey asked.

"It's not enough," Everlie shook her head, "someone needs to actually be *in* there to stop me."

Everlie collapsed against the steering wheel, the moonlight framing her dark hair in a silver shadow. Mikey just stared at her.

"I'm crazy, right?" she asked him, her mouth squashed against the wheel, "between those hours, it was totally silent for you, right?"

"O... Of course it was," Mikey gulped, violently shaking his head, "I didn't hear anything."

Everlie's shoulders relaxed as a cloud of pent-up tension left her body.

"Thank you," she sighed, stroking Mikey's hand as her head stayed resting on the steering wheel, "thank you, Mikey."

Mikey watched the sad girl in silence.

"Listen, why don't we go inside for a bit, eh?" Mikey suggested eventually, "did that internet router come?"

"Yeah, it came," Everlie laughed, clearing herself up, "I've still got no idea how to set it up though."

"Well, I can show you, eh?" Mikey smiled, patting her on the leg, "it might be a chance to forget about all this for a while."

"You're not tired?"

Mikey checked the time. On the dashboard, the clock flashed: 1:15.

"Not yet," he said, pulling the door handle and stepping out.

*

Setting up the internet router by candlelight was weirdly cosy. Mikey was about to blow them out and turn on the lights, but Everlie stopped him.

"The smell helps me relax," she hushed, half slumped on the living room couch with Wicca sitting in her lap, "is that okay?"

"Sure," Mikey obliged while tapping in the Wi-Fi code into his phone.

The word of 'Fail Army' and pet videos had been a whole new experience for Everlie as the pair sat on the couch, with Mikey holding out his phone so they both could watch. As Mikey put on a curated playlist of his favourites (dubbed 'Mikey's Dumb Videos') Everlie giggled alongside him as her cheeks dimpled in delight.

"Where has this been all my life?" she muttered in a sleepy haze halfway through 'Watch People Die Inside Vol.4'.

As the video ended and the 'Subscribe and Like for more' window popped up, Mikey turned to his dozing companion.

"Want to watch another one?" he whispered, turning to her.

She didn't answer.

"Everlie?"

She was asleep, with her head resting gently on his shoulder.

Mikey squirmed on the couch. Could he get up without waking her? Mikey tried to rise, but her head weighed down on him like a watermelon. Next to him, Wicca looked up from Everlie's lap and sniffed his hand. Mikey twitched a smile as he reciprocated, scratching the beast's head as the candlelight flickered in her marble eyes. Was the puss finally starting to like him? Resigned, Mikey sank deeper into the cushion. Damn, this sofa was comfy, maybe he could just spend the night here?

But no, it was getting late. Mikey checked the clock on his phone (his background was still a picture of Amy) and he caught the time. It was 01:48, almost 2am. Mikey decided he needed to stay true to his promise to Everlie whether she was asleep or not.

Squeezing his head out from under Everlie's mass, Mikey managed to climb out while Everlie's head stuck to the backrest. However, just as he started to tiptoe towards the door, Wicca meowed impatiently.

"Shhh!" Mikey scolded the cat.

But Wicca leapt off Everlie's lap and hurried off into the kitchen. Surely *that* would have woken Everlie up. But no, the girl only stirred slightly, her body sitting lopsidedly on the couch, showing Mikey the gape of her cleavage. Mikey turned away, his cheeks burning.

"Goodnight Everlie," he hushed as he left the living room, blowing out the nearby candle on his way.

Behind him, in the dark, Everlie's eyes shot open and followed Mikey, making sure he was going upstairs as he'd been told.

*

Shutting his bedroom door quietly in the dark, Mikey butted his head softly against it.

"Do not start liking her," he commanded himself, eyes shut, "do NOT start liking her."

But it was already too late. Despite every weird thing she'd put him through, Mikey was feeling a familiar itch. It had been a while since he'd felt a female's warmth, and chunky goth weirdos weren't usually his type, but here he was. Tiptoeing back to his bed, he blinked his eyes rapidly.

'Stop it brain,' he scolded himself, '*stop* it!'

But the runaway train of Mikey's base, logic-free emotions were charging ahead and soon the rest of his body would follow, *every* part. All he could do was try to get to sleep and hope he forgot about these stray, intoxicating feelings in the morning.

Stripping down to his boxers, Mikey lifted the dainty, cotton frills of Maddy's bed sheets and slipped under them. After their conversation earlier, Mikey now understood a bit more why Everlie didn't want this room altered, she clearly wasn't over what had happened.

But maybe Maddy wasn't really gone.

"Don't be silly, I just had a bad dream last night," he grunted out loud, pulling up the sheet.

The cool weight of the duvet fell onto him, and Mikey wondered if he and Everlie were *both* going crazy. After all, they were two misfit twenty-somethings drifting through the 2020's with no direction and were now stuck in a big dark house together. Surely, it was enough to make anyone start hearing ghosts. Even then, Everlie had more of an excuse than Mikey. At least she'd been *close* to the girl who had died...

Perhaps Maddy and Everlie had been *more* than just friends: two secret childhood sweethearts, one a fan of Taylor Swift, the other a dedicated goth, living alone together with no internet or social life to speak of. Combined with the recent pandemic lockdown, it was the perfect storm for a forbidden romance to start blossoming.

The thought sent a swift surge of warmth down to Mikey's crotch.

"Urgh, stop it," Mikey groaned as he turned onto his side, clamping the ends of a baby pink pillows over his head, "I do NOT need any more weirdness in my life *or* in my head. Please!"

The mantra repeated in Mikey's brain until he drifted off to sleep, safe in the knowledge that, in his heart of hearts, he didn't believe in ghosts and wouldn't hear any strange noises tonight. In fact, he felt desperately sorry for the girl downstairs, so wrought with grief that she was starting to believe such things....

Poor Everlie, poor poor Everlie...

*

But later that night, Mikey was again woken up by the sound of crying.

8

Chapter 7

The sound was unmistakable: pained, wet, and retching. It was coming from under the bed.

Mikey, now wide awake, threw off the duvet and darted for the door. Wearing only his boxers, he broke into a sweat in the late summer night air and rattled the thick iron handle with both hands. Locked, and Mikey didn't even need to check to know what time it was.

"Shit," Mikey squeaked, biting his knuckles, his eyes flitting around the dark room for something to make into a weapon, "shit shit SHIT!"

The floorboards behind him creaked. The thing under the bed was now on its feet.

"Please..." the sniffling, floaty female voice begged him as her footsteps came closer, "leave me alone..."

Heart racing, and seeing nothing before him but a hairbrush and an old teddy bear on the desk by the door, Mikey felt a cold breath tickling the nape of his neck.

"Please..." the ghostly voice whimpered again, stirring the goosebumps on Mikey's flesh, "leave me alone... I don't want to talk to you..."

Squeezing his eyes shut, Michael summoned a deep, chilly breath.

'Don't be a pussy,' he commanded himself, 'be a MAN!'

"M... Maddy?" he forced the word out of his throat, fists clenched at his sides, "is that your name?"

The footsteps stopped. Dream or not, this strategy seemed to have done something.

"H... How do you know my name?" was all the faint voice could manage, "who are you?"

"Maddy," Mikey pushed on, swallowing, "I just want you to know that... It's okay. You can rest now."

Silence. Mikey's heart knocked against his chest. Was it over? Could he wake up now? No, Mikey still could still hear breathing. Actually, it was more like the breathing of an angry dog.

"O-*kay*!?" The voice wailed, "How can this *ever* be okay?"

"Maddy..."

"It can never be okay," the ghostly voice screamed at him, "NEVER!"

The sound made the hairs on Mikey's back stand rigid. Fists clenched, Mikey swung around and squared out his shoulders, ready to smack whoever this was, girl, ghost, or *whatever*, right upside the head.

However, what he saw stopped him.

The apparition was everything Mikey imagined a ghost would look like: deathly-pale skin, ghost white hair, and cloudy cataracts covering her gaze. The presence was translucent, revealing the back wall behind her, but solid enough for Mikey to identify the shape of a young woman wearing clothes surely meant for someone far younger: a puffy yellow coat covered a pink t-shirt, which was patterned with the kind of love hearts and cartoon cats that would have gone perfectly with Mikey's bed sheets. A pair of knitted mittens hung from clips on the apparition's coat sleeves, with a matching bobble hat sitting on her head. The front of her coat had been slashed, spilling clumps of reddened wool, and the girl's white skin was marked with splotches of dried blood.

And then there was her face.

Hers were not the features of an ordinary young woman; her jaw was far too protruding, and her nose resembled something close to a snout. These features resembled something closer to the head of a predatory animal than a human. Before Mikey could scream, the apparition pounced on him. Mikey raised his hands as the thing bit down hard on his arm...

*

Mikey woke up screaming.

Chest heaving, Mikey saw that he was only wearing his boxers, but otherwise everything was a mirror image of the previous morning: daylight streamed in through the bedroom window, he was sitting with his back propped against the door, and he was soaking wet. Only this time, the dark, sticky stuff pooling at his crotch and crusting his arm to his chest was burgundy red and smelt like copper. Mikey's arm ached as he lifted it.

"Jesus..." he gasped, throwing his hand over his mouth, "Jesus fucking Christ..."

Red and raw, the gash circled his arm and was dotted with deep, stinging grooves that were still weeping.

"Fuck..." Mikey whimpered, heart hammering, "fuck fuck fuck-fuckfuck..."

It was a bite mark.

Chapter 8

"Everlie, wake up!"

Everlie had been lying in the hallway outside his bedroom door when he opened it and shouted at her, and Mikey found himself wondering if anybody in this bloody house slept in their own beds at night.

"Mnn, what?" she groaned, rubbing her eyes.

Everlie had the resting face of someone who'd gone to bed pissed-off and woken up about the same. Presumably, her 'personal project' had gone about as well as the night previously.

However, she became wide awake when she saw the bite mark on Mikey's arm.

"Whoa, what happened to you?" she muttered seriously, looking between the gash marks and Mikey's angry face as she slid herself back up the wall.

"You tell me!" he snapped at her, holding his arm out, "I didn't do this to myself!"

On her feet, Everlie didn't seem to hear him. She just stared at the wound in wide eyed fascination.

"Are these..." she trembled, taking Mikey's arm in her hands, "are these *teeth* marks?"

"What is going on, Everlie?" Mikey yanked his arm away before she could study it any further, "tell me the truth!"

Everlie just shook her head, blinking rapidly, trying to knock the fog from her brain.

"I... I don't know..." she slurred, tripping over her tongue, "I mean, NOTHING!"

Inhaling deeply through his nose, Mikey stepped away from her, shaking his head as he stormed back into his room to pick up his kit bags.

"What are you doing?" Everlie asked, creeping into the doorway.

Mikey didn't answer. He collected his things from around the room and stuffed them into his bag.

"Are you leaving?" Everlie pressed, walking closer, "you're not leaving, are you?"

After winding up the power lead, Mikey turned to lay his laptop on his messily gathered clothes, only to miss as his kit bag was pulled away from him. Mikey looked up to see Everlie, hunched over with both hands on his bag, which was now pulled close to her chest. She was looking right at him.

"You can't leave," she told him seriously, "Not yet."

"Why not?" he reeled, grabbing his bag at the other end, "What aren't you telling me!?"

Everlie didn't answer but tried to yank the bag away again. Finally losing it, Mikey used both arms to pull it off her, sending Everlie skidding along the room's glazed wood flooring on her knees.

"I told you everything yesterday!" Everlie cried up at him as he slung the bag over his shoulder, "please, you have to believe me Mikey!"

Mikey shook his head. He didn't believe her, and he was sick of letting himself get manipulated.

"Goodbye Everlie," Mikey declared as he stormed out of the bedroom door.

"NO!"

As Mikey made it to the top of the stairs, Everlie was barrelling after him, bouncing off the walls as she called out his name.

"Mikey, Wait! I promise I don't know what bit you," Everlie pleaded, choking on her desperation, "but please just *listen* to me. PLEASE!"

Mikey kept going. He was halfway down the stairs, the front door in sight, when Everlie made a grab for his shoulder. Everlie had been trying to pull Mikey around to make him face her, but she ended up tugging his shirt too hard and made his left foot slip off the stairs. Everlie was now caught between trying to hold onto him and keeping herself steady, which led to her toppling over too. Then, they both went tumbling down the stairs. Everlie, curled up into a ball, was bitten by each step on her way down before rolling to a stop, while Mikey ended up using his bag as a makeshift sled (the crunch of his laptop screen all too audible as it took the brunt of his weight).

After two seconds in freefall, the duo crash landed in the messy hallway, groaning, and rubbing their bruises. Raising himself on both arms, Mikey hooked his fingers around the dangling handle of his bag, the rattle of the broken contents making him wince. Meanwhile, behind him, Everlie was making a grab for the cuff of his jeans. On pure instinct, Mikey kicked out with his other leg and hit her squarely in the face. There was a brittle crunch as Mikey's trainer connected with her noise. Noiselessly, Everlie recoiled and threw her hand up to her face.

"Oh... shit," Mikey gasped, "sorry Everlie."

Not quite fully believing what he'd done, Mikey rode through the pain of the fall and scrambled to his feet with his kit bag now tucked under his arms.

"Everlie... I didn't mean to do that," he hushed, "are... are you okay?"

Everlie said nothing, she just sat holding her nose as blood dribbled through her fingers, almost as if she was doing her best to keep it stuck to her face. Mikey tried to make another apology when a muffled honking noise cut him off. It was a graceless sound, full of agony and despair, which sent Mikey further towards the door.

"I'm sorry, Everlie," Mikey apologised finally, almost on the verge of tears himself.

There was so much more he wanted to say and to ask, but he couldn't. All he could do was repeat himself.

"I'm sorry," he offered one last time before shouldering his bags and fled out the door, leaving the utterly defeated Everlie sitting alone in her dark house, crying her eyes out.

Chapter 9

In the coffee shop, Mikey held his arm out in front of him, fascinated by the wound. It was still bleeding. The punctures were rugged and nasty, but he felt he'd gotten away easy compared to the set of teeth which had left them there. He remembered the ghostly apparition, dressed like a normal young woman, whose jaw had pulled him like a chew toy.

"Mikey," the voice across the table said, "are you listening to me?"

Mikey's eyes shot up and he returned to the surroundings of the coffee shop. Across from him, his ex-girlfriend Amy wrung both hands around her latte, squeezing the mug.

"Sorry," Mikey laughed nervously, "I zoned out there."

"It's alright," she sighed patiently, flicking a loose strand of auburn hair out of her face as she leaned across the table, "just tell me again, slowly, what exactly happened in that house?"

Mikey wiped a hand down his stubbly face. He felt like a living zombie. His fight with Everlie had left him with nowhere to go, so he'd had no choice but to call Amy. His adrenaline was now fully spent, and his bruised body was punishing him worse than any late-night hangover. Even the espresso hadn't helped.

Mikey told her everything again, barring the sight of Maddy's ghost.

"Goodness," Amy shook her head, shocked, "so, how did you get the bite?"

Mikey quickly took his arm off the table.

"Oh, I... I don't really know," Mikey shied away, "I think Everlie might have done it."

"Listen, Mikey, I'm sorry that happened to you," Amy patted his hand, "but unless you saw her do it, I can't help you prove anything."

"Are you saying you don't believe me?" Mikey looked up at her.

"No," Amy winced, shaking her head, "no, I'm not saying that."

"I don't want to stay quiet about this Amy," Mikey pleaded, "I could be in danger from her!"

"Listen, Mikey," Amy approached softly, like she was about to give him some bad news, "why don't you come back and stay with me for a night or two, okay?"

Mikey's face lit up.

"However," she sighed, "we probably have to discuss a few things first."

Mikey's hands gripped the edge of the table as he braced himself for what was next.

"I'm sorry for upsetting you Amy," he grimaced, not looking at her.

Amy didn't exactly look happy. Mikey rolled his eyes.

"I accept, but just about you upsetting me," Amy tucked her hands in her lap, hiding behind her fringe, "you need to understand *why* I was upset, okay?"

Mikey tapped his feet and clenched his teeth.

"It's not that difficult, Mikey," Amy told him calmly, "please."

Mikey clawed his nails against the table.

"Amy, I..." he began, looking up at her.

And he was stopped by her beauty: auburn hair cascading down her hair in floaty waves, her soft, mocha-toned skin, and her wide eyes that expressed sensitivity and understanding. How the hell was Mikey to blame for not wanting more sex with *that*? Ever since he'd first met her, Mikey had been able to make Amy laugh, but she'd also been constantly frigid for no other reason than the conservative, religious upbringing her parents had forced upon her. All Mikey had been trying to do was make her realise that they could just be like a normal couple. Was that so wrong?

"All I did was put my arm around you and you went mental!" Mikey wined, struggling to maintain eye contact with her.

"Put your arm around me?" Amy receded, once again using her fringe as cover, "You grabbed my arse!"

"I... I slipped, honest!" Mikey put his hand on his face and slumped over the table, "I'm sorry, okay?"

"I'd already told you I didn't want it," Amy shook her head sadly.

'You *never* want it!' Mikey wanted to scream, panic and male pride taking over.

But no. He couldn't lose her again.

They both went silent, looking away from each other. The nattering around the shop seemed to fade out around them. In front of her, Amy's latte had gone cold.

"Look," Amy sighed, "maybe we shouldn't even be together."

Fear seized Mikey's heart as he looked up from the floor.

"But I *do* want to be with you Amy," Mikey blubbered, wringing his hands, "I love you!"

Amy seemed to think about it for a moment.

"But can you be comfortable with what I can't give you?" Amy shrugged sadly, "even if it's not 'normal' by your standards."

"Okay…"

"Are you just saying that?" Amy cut in, now looking up at him, "are you still feeling sorry for yourself?"

Mikey folded his arms and looked away. He *did* feel sorry for himself, and he hated that she always noticed it.

'Just lie,' Mikey told himself, the fearful thought repeating in his mind, *'just lie, and everything will go back to how it was.'*

"No," Mikey gulped, not looking at her, "I'm not just saying it, Amy. I mean it. I want to be with you, no matter what."

Looking up at him, Amy managed a smile.

"Okay," she hushed, flicking a strand of hair away from her face, "Well, let's get going then, people are staring at us."

Their plastic chairs shrieked as Mikey followed her sheepishly to the door, collecting their rubbish from the table and dumping it in the bin on his way out. Amy smiled and thanked the staff as she left. Mikey did not.

*

'Home sweet home,' Mikey thought as Amy opened the door and let him inside.

"Quick," she ushered, flecks of rain hitting her, "get inside."

Mikey hurried out from the impending August shower and into the safety of his old front hallway. Next to the front door was the living room, his TV with his DVD collection sitting in the far corner. Beyond that was the kitchen with its soft yellow lighting and tiled surfaces making it the one nice looking place in the whole house. Everything was exactly as he'd left it.

"So," Amy shrugged, turning back to him, "what are we eating?"

"Oh, shit," Mikey scratched the nape of his neck, having honestly forgotten about food, "what have you got?"

"Leftovers," Amy chuckled half-heartedly and motioned to the kitchen.

The offer hung limply in the air for a second or two.

"Takeout?" Mikey asked hopefully.

"Takeout," Amy agreed with a relieved smile.

At 6pm, their pizzas arrived, which they ate at opposite ends of the sofa.

"And you say she didn't have any internet?" Amy asked from across the couch, a black olive almost rolling off her slice as it dangled by her face, "like, at *all*?"

"She said it was for her mental health, or something," Mikey shook his head tightly with his arms crossed over his pizza box, not really wanting to talk about it.

The gash on his arm suddenly throbbed under the bandage.

"I guess so," Amy pondered as she took a small bite out of her slice.

Mikey tried to distract Amy from any further questions about Poppygrow House by broadcasting some funny videos from his phone onto the TV (he still had Amy's Wi-Fi code saved). Before long, she was giggling at them while stifling her food filled mouth with her hand. Mikey smiled as his gaze wandered over to her, it was just like old times.

'You're on a roll here, mate,' he encouraged himself, tracking Amy's enjoyment, 'keep it up!'

Unfortunately, the final video in Mikey's 'Dumb Videos' collection, 'Spongebob Squarepants sings the hits of Cliff Richard', turned out to be a bit of a dud.

"I don't really get this AI music gimmick," Amy shrugged, returning to her food, "if you know the original song, it's all you can hear."

"Oh yeah?" Mikey asked, stifling his own amusement.

"Are you kidding, my parents forced Cliff's music on me growing up," Amy scoffed, "the man is practically extended family."

Mikey squinted with his ears, honestly having difficulty hearing it.

"You can really tell, huh?" Mikey looked up at her.

"Of course!" Amy laughed, "the heart and soul of a voice, the tone and personality, can't be masked."

"I've gotta say, I can't really tell," Mikey chided, scratching his ear, "but my parents' had better music taste than yours."

This made Amy giggle again.

Before long, it started to get late. Amy was sitting pensively at the other end of the coach, deliberating the same thing Mikey was.

"I'll sleep in here tonight," Mikey slipped the suggestion in first.

"Right," Amy shot off the couch, relieved, "I'll get your bedding,"

Mikey used the moment to brush his teeth in the downstairs bathroom, his brush still standing in the stained glass by the sink. Back in the living room, Amy lay out the blanket and a single pillow.

"Thanks," Mikey obliged, taking off his shoes.

"Don't mention it," Amy wandered over to the light switch by the door.

She waited there for a while, her finger hovering over the switch. Mikey slipped under the covers with his jeans still on.

"Something wrong?" Mikey asked, propping himself up with one arm.

Amy seemed to think about it for a second before shaking her head.

"Nothing, nothing at all," she sighed, flicking off the switch, "goodnight, Mikey."

"Goodnight," he replied, dropping back down, "lo…"

He cut himself off.

'She probably didn't hear me,' Mikey tried to convince himself as he sank down against the pillow, trying to ignore the blinking red standby switch on the television, 'she probably didn't hear…'

*

A muffled noise rose Mikey from sleep in the middle of the night. This time, he remembered exactly where he was. Amy's living room felt more like home than anywhere else he'd been staying recently.

Mikey checked his watch, 2:05am.

'No crying tonight,' he thought to himself, turning over on the sofa, 'no bloody ghosts either, thank God...'

But as he became more awake, Mikey took more notice of the sound drifting down from the upstairs bedroom where he and Amy used to sleep together.

It sounded like a pained, human noise, the sound of crying.

Maddy had found him again.

Chapter 10

"No way!" Mikey almost screamed as he sat up on the sofa, "Just... No!"

It shouldn't have been possible. Mikey was *away* from Poppygrow House, away from Maddy! And yet, somehow, her presence had followed him here.

Mikey's racing thoughts automatically homed in on an old film he'd seen with Amy once, *The Grudge,* a haunted house flick about a place that cursed you upon merely stepping foot in it, and no matter what you did, you could never escape.

"It can't be like that," Mikey muttered, shaking his head with his hands over his eyes, "it's impossible!"

Yet the sound was unmistakable, just as it had been the previous two nights. The wailing floated down the stairs from the second floor, beckoning him.

"No," Mikey repeated, throwing himself back into the sofa and jamming a pillow over his ears, "not this time."

Burying his face against the sofa, Mikey decided that tonight he would just ignore the crying until it stopped. Even if that sniffling, wet voice came close enough for him to feel its frigid breath on his skin, he wouldn't pay attention to it. Surely, a ghost couldn't hurt him if he just refused to acknowledge it.

But the black bite mark on his arm started to throb, flaring up in a hot sting. He could feel the puncture marks in the skin bleeding again, forcing Mikey to grasp it painfully and sit up. Sweating and panting, Mikey watched the wound. It was soaking the gauze. The ghostly weeping seemed to be reaching out to it, summoning it, and inviting Mikey along for the ride. If he wanted the pain to subside, Mikey couldn't refuse its call.

"But not without protection," Mikey gritted his teeth, wiping a layer of sweat off his face, "I'm not *that* stupid."

Mikey got to his feet and instantly noticed how a new fever had fallen on him. If it wasn't for the bitter cold of the tiled kitchen floor against his toes as he opened the drawer and pulled out a large kitchen knife, he might have completely burned up. The serrated edge of Mikey's blade shimmered in the silver moonlight.

Upstairs, the crying continued.

'I'm coming,' Mikey breathed, the air growing colder as he tucked the knife into the back of his trousers, 'keep your knickers on.'

As he ascended the stairs, the wailing became louder and louder with each trembling step. At every sound, Mikey found himself looking over the banister to check for anything trying to sneak up on him from above.

'What if it's Amy?' Mikey thought in a moment of panic, 'how will it look, me coming upstairs brandishing a knife while she's crying her eyes out?'

But no, Mikey knew better. He knew painfully well what Amy's crying sounded like, and this wasn't it.

'That's why I came prepared,' he reminded himself, feeling for the kitchen knife tucked in the back of his trousers as he reached the landing, 'Mikey Howes ain't afraid of no *fucking* ghost!"

As expected, the sound of the crying was coming from Amy's room, *their* old room. The door was ajar. Swallowing dryly, Mikey gently pushed the door back and saw Maddy, on her knees, weeping.

However, this wasn't what sent Mikey reeling against the inner wall.

"Jesus..." he gasped, putting his hand over his mouth.

There was a single bed with frilly pink covers, a torn-up poster sitting in the far corner, and teddy bears sitting atop the wardrobe to his left. This wasn't Amy's room; Mikey had somehow stepped *back* into Poppygrow House. The dead girl was sitting in the centre of the room, exactly where she'd been last night, with her back to him as she cried into her mittens.

"I don't want to talk to her..." Maddy sobbed, wiping her face with her bloody hands, "why can't she understand that? Why can't *Everlie* understand that?"

With his back pressed against the pink wall, digging the blunt edge of the knife against his buttock, Mikey shut his eyes and took a deep breath as he prepared to reach out. He wasn't sure how, but he had to try and end this.

"Maddy?" He asked.

Instantly, the spirit was on her feet and facing him, revealing her ripped coat with bloody clumps of down feathers spilling out of the front. She held her stained hands out to him pleadingly. Mikey's heart pounded as he noticed her form was more solid than last night, barely letting any light through this time.

"Everlie's outside my room right now, isn't she? She's still trying to perform the ritual," Maddy told him, her face taut with panic, "it won't work, *you* need to be there."

Mikey's hands scraped the wallpaper as he stayed pressed against it. The tips of his fingers started to freeze as Maddy came close to grasping them.

"But why me?" Mikey blubbered, feeling Maddy's cold breath as it steamed in the air, even on this sticky hot night.

"Because you're the conduit," she explained, practically in his face now, "she chose *you*."

Mikey was trapped by the eyes of this dead girl, her glassy stare pinning him to the wall. Up close, her features didn't quite hold the rabid, dog-like hunger they had shown the night previously. Yet.

"Listen, I... I'm so sorry about what happened to you Maddy," Mikey licked his frozen lips, "but I don't understand any of this..."

"Don't either of you get it?!" She then screamed, making him jump, "I'm dead now, the Dark is drawing me in! There's no going back."

"The *Dark?*" Mikey stammered, pulling away, "what do you mean?"

Maddy's ghost rushed forward, grasping Mikey's hands. Mikey felt a bolt of numbing pain shoot through him, settling on the gash in his arm which now throbbed mercilessly.

"Listen to me, the more times Everlie tries to contact me, the more of the Dark I bring with me," she clenched her fists, hurting him, "That's why I can't talk to her, I'm trying to *protect* her!"

Unable to look Maddy in the eyes, Mike's gaze flitted up over her shoulder. He saw something: right next to Maddy's bed, just to the right of the love-heart imprinted headboard, there was a black spot growing on the wall. At first, Mikey thought it was mould, but he quickly realised that it was growing outwards, getting bigger with each passing second. In seconds, the large black spot was so deep and black that Mikey couldn't even focus on it. A whirlpool of darkness.

His wound, the one Maddy had given him with her razor teeth last night, was suddenly throbbing and pulsing with the rhythm of his thudding heart. As the blotch on the wall grew, so too did the black stain on his bandage, like the blood was being drawn out of it. Mikey winced, biting down.

"Let me go," Mikey begged Maddy's ghost, "please... I just want my old life back..."

Maddy pulled him closer. As he locked eyes with the white faced, staring girl, Mikey noticed a strange black mist dancing before his face. Blood, his *own* blood. It was spiralling through the air as if in zero gravity, being pulled from his body towards the growing dark hole across the room.

Mikey became transfixed, chasing the stream with his eyes until it led him to the centre of the portal. Looking closer, Mikey realised with sharp dread that this void was not empty. There was something *in* there. Mikey heard noises that sounded to him like snapping teeth and writhing claws, digging to get out. Whatever was beyond the widening portal was hungry. *Very* hungry.

"What is that?" Mikey swallowed dryly, pointing a trembling finger at the blotch, "what the *fuck* is that?"

"The Dark," Maddy answered.

She uttered it with such gentle finality that Mikey didn't fully realise the danger until he turned back to Maddy and saw that her eyes, face, and nose were not her own anymore. Mikey was staring at the face of a predator.

Maddy screamed, launching her dagger teeth at him.

"NO!"

In the grip of animal terror, Mikey ripped himself from Maddy's grasp. He pulled the handle of the knife in his belt, but the serrated edges got caught on his belt strap. With one arm trapped behind his back, Maddy's snout landed on his upper chest, ravaging his skin. As Maddy bit and tore, Mikey pushed off the wall. Landing on her, Mikey made another grasp for the knife while Maddy's horrible, contorted face gnashed and snapped while she lay trapped under his weight. Mikey wielded the kitchen knife above her and prepared to plunge down...

*

"Mikey!!" Amy's voice wailed, waking him up, "what on Earth are you doing!?"

The sound made Mikey freeze as he stopped the knife in mid-air. Startled, he swung his head from left to right. No void, no monsters, no Maddy, and the gash on his arm had returned to its previous size. He was in Amy's room, and everything was totally dark. The knife fell harmlessly from his weak fingers onto Amy's bed.

"What the..." Mikey panted, his eyes darting left and right, "who the..."

As he returned to his senses, Mikey knew that only one holdover from his terrible dream remained: there was the weight of a woman trapped under his thighs.

Mikey stared down at the wide, frightened eyes of the woman he'd once wanted to make his wife. The blade of the dropped knife had been inches from her face. Her breath was racing.

"Mikey?" she asked fearfully, "what the fuck are you doing?"

Mikey couldn't answer.

12

Chapter 11

"Amy, wait, let me explain..."

But the door slammed in his face, Mikey found himself out in the cold for the second time in as many weeks. However, this time he wasn't even wearing any shoes!

"Fuck," Mikey gasped, chewing his knuckles, and whirling dizzily on the spot, "fuck fuckfuckfuck!"

Mikey felt like screaming, raging, and whimpering all at once, but ultimately knew none of it would help.

"Amy!" he banged on the front door, "PLEASE LET ME IN!"

Bad idea. Amy was now probably *more* likely to call the police. Mikey returned to pacing in circles on the door stop, chewing his nails as he waited in vain for the white noise of pure adrenaline and panic to pass.

'Get away from here!' the disaffected voice of reason in the back of his mind told him, 'Amy probably doesn't want to see the guy who just held a knife to her face, you know?'

But Mikey had nowhere else to go. The porch light hanging outside Amy's front door was his only beacon of sanctuary left in this rotten world.

"Why me?" Mikey whimpered, hugging himself as he broke away, tearing down the street wearing nothing but his pyjamas, "why always ME!"

This had to be a dream, just like the horrible sleepwalking dream which had made him attack Amy in the first place.

Mikey tried not to cry as he walked alone, away from Amy's house, down the concrete sidewalk which nipped his bare feet. He didn't have his wallet, phone, or anything. Brian's place was too far away, so he'd probably need to find a bridge to sleep under or something.

'No way!' he shook his head, staring at the ground as he walked, 'I can't be homeless, I'm not on drugs or anything like that!'

But it wasn't that simple, and he knew it. In this world, *anyone* could become homeless. It didn't only happen to 'certain people' anymore. If a directionless scrub like Mikey could somehow graduate from university and briefly land a gorgeous girlfriend like Amy Russell without anyone noticing, then surely the world could make him homeless just as easily.

The one last place Mikey could think of going was back to Poppy-grow House. Looking down, he finally started to notice the itchy pain on his upper chest as blood soaked his collar. Mikey shook his head and hugged himself tighter.

'Not in a million years,' he repeated in his head, 'not in a million...'

But at that moment, a stray beam of light caught him. Stopping in his tracks, Mikey stumbled and shielded his eyes.

"There you are," a nasally, squished voice called out to him, "stop right there Mikey!"

Speak of the fishnet-wearing, emo haircut-styled devil.

Mikey dropped his arm and squinted to see a familiar stout, portly young woman with shoulder length raven hair and fishnet sleeves. Everlie had a fresh white plaster stuck across the bridge of her nose.

"Oh fuck," Mikey moaned as Everlie marched towards him, "not YOU again!"

With the torch swinging in her hand, Mikey could barely bring himself to move as Everlie started running.

'Not again,' he resolved, making a break for the park across the road, 'not again!'

"Wait!" Everlie called after him.

Mikey could already hear how out of breath she was. The tarmac nipped Mikey's bare soles as he made for the grassy park just beyond the small row of bushes. Maybe the dewy grass and mud would soothe his feet. However, after narrowly dodging the remnants of a discarded bottle, his right toe caught the curb and he went to the floor, banging his knee.

"Ouch!" he seethed, clutching his leg as he rolled around on the sidewalk.

"Stay there!" Everlie demanded as she came running over, already halfway across the road.

But then a car came swinging into view, honking as it caught Everlie on the tip of its bonnet. Mikey saw his chance, getting to his feet and riding through the pain. He vaulted over the bushes into the nearby park and waited, hidden from sight. After the driver had finished yelling at Everlie, Mikey stayed down, listening to the pitter patter of her feet searching him out.

"Mikey!" Her cry became softer and softer, "Mikeeeeeey!"

Finally, silence.

Mikey waited under the bushes for a while, curled up in a foetal position while the brambles pricked and poked him. Was it okay to peek out yet? Peering out through a gap in the leaves, Mikey couldn't tell if she was gone, but he got to his feet and kept running anyway.

Not looking back, Mikey limped across the grassy park towards the river. If Mikey had truly lost his pursuer, maybe he could dip his legs over the embankment and soothe his aching feet in the water for a bit.

Mikey slid on his bottom down an embankment until the riverside path materialised beneath him. It was dark, but he could hear the babbling water nearby. A few metres to his right was a bridge underpass. It had a dim, blue light for pedestrians, which might have even been useful had it not been spray painted over by some opportunistic graffiti artist.

Using the faint light, Mikey took himself to the edge of the river and sat down, careful not to fall in. He doused his feet in the stream. The cool stream on his burning soles felt good. Even if Everlie caught up to him now, at least he'd be able to enjoy this moment. Mikey shut his eyes and lay back on the wet grass, savouring it. The late August night air was nice and breezy too...

"Oi mate," an angry voice emerged, "you get an invitation or summin'?"

Mikey knew he was in trouble before he even had a chance to see who was talking to him. Closing in were three kids, the blue light from the bridge casting shadows down their hooded faces. The one in the middle was holding a clear sandwich bag filled with some kind of green herb. Mikey guessed it wasn't oregano.

"Listen... don't mind me fellas," Mikey attempted, getting to his feet, and raising his arms in surrender, "I didn't see anything..."

The lead kid, the one clutching the bag, came forward and punched him. Mikey was knocked backwards, holding his stomach.

"What did you do that for?" the kid flanking Mikey's right asked the attacker.

"So he won't go grassing," the attacker replied, shaking his fist.

"I won't... tell anyone," Mikey wheezed, clutching his stomach.

"Not after I'm done with 'ya," the leader then grunted, socking Mikey in the chin.

The kid's small fist sent a shockwave up Mikey's face, rattling his brain. From the leader's voice alone, Mikey could tell the boy wasn't interested in whether Mikey was going to grass on them or not. This was merely 'baby's first drug deal', and this kid clearly wanted to cement his 'badman' status by taking on a bigger lad.

Instead of falling in the river, Mikey quashed the pain and steadied his posture. He wanted to just topple over and fall asleep forever, even if these kids started kicking him in his sleep, but he needed to get to safety first. Summoning the last of his strength, he shoved his attacker out of the way, and broke into a run towards the underpass.

"Oi!" The lead attacker yelled back as Mikey fled.

Footsteps stamped after Mikey as he stumbled towards the underpass, and he just made it there when a sweeping kick knocked his legs out from under him. In seconds, the kids were on him. Two of them savagely kicked Mikey in his chest, arms, and head while he lay on his front with his hands cupped over his head. Meanwhile, the leader's little buddy showed symbolic support, gently dabbing Mikey with his toe.

"Come on guys, this is so dumb," the third boy hung back, impatiently checking around, "he's just some loser, let's just leave him alone."

"What are you, some kind of pussy?" The leader withdrew from Mikey's half-corpse and went over to his friend.

Mikey just lay on the ground (the flanker gave him one last poke and spat on the back of his head for good measure), grateful for the brief reprieve. Muscles aching, Mikey twisted his head to watch the unfolding drama through his swollen eyes.

"I'm just the bloke who sells you weed," the lone pacifist chuckled, hands still in his pocket, "and if you're going to be trouble, I can sell elsewhere."

Mikey's attacker seemed to be thinking about this enough to drop his guard before an overhead siren sent them all scattering, leaving Mikey alone on the ground beneath the underpass.

Silence. Mikey couldn't feel his arms. All over, his muscles tingled. He prayed those yobs hadn't broken any bones, but he didn't feel like moving to find out.

So, this was it then, he was going to be spending the night lying in an underpass? Already in a half-dazed state, Mikey wasn't sure he cared anymore. Dragging himself along the gravel with his one working arm, Mikey tried to tuck himself between the gravelly floor and the graffiti strewn wall next to him. The faint blue light above was his only companion.

"At least things can't get any worse," he grumbled through a mouthful of blood.

But that was when he heard slow footsteps coming up behind him.

Dragging his swollen cheek across the ground, Mikey turned his head to check those kids weren't coming back for him. They weren't, but he now wished they were.

There was someone coming, his features were doused in shadow, save for a faded blue Macintosh which drifted out of the night towards him.

"You've heard her," a rusty voice asked from the darkness, "haven't you?"

CHAPTER 12

"Fuck!" Mikey panicked, spitting out blood as he held his trembling arm towards the old man, "stay away from me you fucking CREEP!"

The old man just kept walking; his bare feet soundless against the ground as they left muddy footprints in his wake. The staring eyes in the man's withered old face trapped Mikey with their glare.

"I'm not going to hurt you," the old man said, his speech low and floaty.

'Yeah, like FUCK!' Mikey thought as he tried to wriggle away, remembering how the old ghoul had tried to bite him last time.

With no strength in his legs, Mikey squirmed away on his front, his bottom rising and falling as he shuffled like a worm, leaving a trail of blood in his wake. However, the old man's gentle footfalls became louder. Soon, Mikey's only exit was blocked by a pair of dirty feet, barely visible in the blue half-light. Their musky smell, however, was a different matter entirely. Mikey retched.

"Listen to me," the old man sighed, ignoring Mikey's struggle, "there is only one way to escape this nightmare."

Mikey wasn't keen to listen to this crazy hermit.

"Pay attention," the old man persisted, "I'm trying to save you."

"S... save me?" Mikey coughed, "from *what*?"

"From making the same mistake I did," the man's voice was smoky and dry, like the cracking of a log fire, "you've heard her, haven't you?"

"Y... yes, okay... maybe I have," Mikey could no longer deny as he lay helplessly on the ground, "what's it to you?"

The old man's knees popped as he bent down, lowering himself to Mikey's eye level. Mikey tried not to look at him.

"Everlie might have told you some tale about 'hearing voices' at night," the man continued, "but she's a liar."

"Listen, what do you want from me!?" Mikey trembled, clenching his eyes shut, "how do you know Everlie?"

"Look at me, young man."

"No..."

"LOOK AT ME!"

Mikey's eyes opened. The face of this old spectre, wiry white beard and hawk nose lit in dark blue, was all he could see. Mikey could pick out every line, every crusty sore, in the man's aged face. His eyes were like black stones. The marks on Mikey's arm and chest began to throb harder in this man's presence, as if drawn to him.

"Listen, I want to tell you my story," The man's rotting breath savaged Mikey, "and you must pay close attention, or you'll never escape the Dark."

Mikey had no choice as the man's hypnotic gaze pulled his tired mind deeper and deeper into sleep.

"W... Who are you?" Mikey croaked.

"My name is Benjamin," the old man said, "and my own nightmare began after the death of my grandmother..."

*

"When I was a boy, I mourned her deeply," Ben began.

"She passed away in the hospital, and I never got a chance to say goodbye. So, my father invented a game to comfort me. This game involved visiting my grandmother's empty house between the hours of three and four in the afternoon, the same hour in which she passed, and told me to wait outside her bedroom door. *Her* room..."

"Before going in himself, my father would instruct me to block the door from the outside and keep my very best memories of her at the forefront of my mind. He told me to concentrate on them with such intensity that everything else faded away. By doing this, I could make her spirit materialise in the room, and I could finally say goodbye..."

"After minutes of waiting, trusting, and searching the depths of my feelings, I finally heard my grandmother's voice from the other side of the door. Of course, it sounded like my father, but the words, tone, and texture could not be denied: it was the voice of my grandmother speaking through him. Thanks to him, I finally got my chance to say goodbye..."

"However, as I grew up, I started to see my father's 'game' for what it really was: a sham. He had been trying to push his dwindling grip of reality onto me, and I refused to let that happen. I would *not* become like him. And so, I ran away from home..."

"Years later, I formed a family of my own. For a while, I was happy...

"But then, my wife passed. Against my better judgement, I used the same ritual which had once soothed me to help my own grieving child. Only then did I discover my father's ritual had been far more than a comforting farce...

"As the nights went by, and despite the increasing resistance, I became addicted to this process. This ritual..."

Oblivious to all else but the presence of the old storyteller and the black vortex staring at him through those hollow eyes, Mikey listened.

"Resistance?" Mikey asked sleepily, "wha..."

Silently, Ben reached into the pocket in his macintosh. Mikey leaned forward to get a better look at what the old man was showing him but was sent reeling when a gleaming blade was pulled out, stopping inches from Mikey's eye. Mikey was frozen in place, staring as the man gave Mikey a better look at his weapon: a one-armed scissor with a glistening, golden coat. The only thing dulling the weapon's shimmering finish was a brown smear caked around the blade which might have been rust, or blood.

With his eyes still fixed on Mikey, Benjamin lifted the blade to the collar of his coat and cut downwards. Shedding layers of old twine and fabric, Benjamin jaggedly sliced the scissor down the front of his macintosh, and let the shredded coat fall to the floor when he was done, revealing his nude figure.

"Jesus CHRIST!" Mikey screamed, placing both hands on his mouth.

The naked man's entire body was covered in bites.

"Listen to me," Ben declared, his eyes baring down on Mikey, "when a person is called back from the dead, they do not return as they once were. They come back tainted by the Dark."

The Dark.

Mikey remembered the word from when he'd been visited by Maddy's spirit. The old man saw this understanding in Mikey's face and nodded.

"Beyond this mortal coil, the Dark is a place of eternal rest and peace for all passing souls drawn to its bosom," the old man whispered to him, unphased by the cold, "but when the Dark is introduced to even a small taste of the living world, it becomes ravenous. Those it infects; it lives on like a parasite."

With a speed that made Mikey gasp, the man lunged down and grabbed Mikey's arm, digging into his flesh with those yellowed nails, and ripped the bandage off his arm. Screaming in horror, Mikey was forced to look at the throbbing black mass that pulsed and oozed on his skin like a bloodsucking leech.

"You have been infected," Ben declared, studying the gash, "Now, the Dark may live inside you forever, as it does me. You will be haunted by visions until the Dark totally consumes your mind..."

"But you can save me, right?" Mikey clawed at Ben's feet, pleading, "right!?"

Ben smiled; an expression darkly familiar to the one he'd seen from the departing car window when Everlie had driven him home that rainy evening.

"Your infection hasn't grown too far yet, so you may still have a chance," the old man's eyes glimmered, "to save yourself, you must interrupt Everlie's next ritual."

Mikey clung to the old man's scar riddled leg, his unkempt pubic bush alarmingly close to his face.

"What do you mean?" Mikey's lips trembled, "interrupt?"

Hungrily, the old man licked his cracked lips.

"The communication ritual is a very fragile process," the man trembled giddily, "if the conditions are broken even slightly, it can never be performed by the same person again. Ever again."

"So... I need to wreck Everlie's next ritual, huh?" Mikey gripped him harder, becoming breathless, "okay... but how? What am I supposed to do?"

The old man said nothing. He just stared down at Mikey with that black, all-consuming gaze that seemed to push away all light from around them.

Finally, Mikey became surrounded by darkness. The aches and pains in his muscles became too great as they dragged him down into unconsciousness and his thoughts were washed away by sleep.

Deep, merciful sleep...
*

When Mikey woke up, he was lying in the underpass.

The fresh morning air stung his nose. Brilliant sunlight stared through the trees across the river. Barely able to move, Mikey groaned and heaved himself along the tarmac until he was sitting against the chilly, concrete wall.

'What happened last night?' he thought, knocking his head back against the wall, 'was it all a dream?'

The bruises and bitter cold were brutal reminders that at least *some* of it had been real. The real question was, what did it mean for him now?

"I have to go to a homeless shelter," Mikey nodded as he pulled his legs up to his chin, "I have to get myself to a..."

And then, he cracked. Mikey burst into tears and sat under the bridge, holding himself in the morning sunshine. How did it come to this?

"This isn't fair," he told himself, wiping the dirty streaks from his face, "I didn't do anything to deserve all this!"

But it wasn't entirely true. At the end of the day, everything came back to one vital decision Mikey had made: moving away from Amy instead of just apologising to her. He knew he'd been wrong to do it now, it had taken being chased across town and a severe beating, physically and emotionally, for him to fully realise it, but now Mikey was truly sorry. Truly *truly* sorry. He now realised that there was far more to life than having sex when he wanted, and far *far* more to love. Mikey now felt he would gladly forsake having sex with anyone or *anything* ever again if it meant spending one more silly evening with Amy, watching videos on their couch together...

Mikey was sorry, but it was far too late.

It was over.

'It might be over,' the rational part of his brain, barely clinging on, said, 'but it's not too late to apologise to her.'

This thought was enough for Mikey to raise himself up against the wall, before immediately collapsing into a limp as his strained leg muscles struggled with the load. It was then that he noticed something fall out of his pocket. Mikey followed the noise and saw, skittering across the ground, that it was a long piece of rusted metal which he didn't recognise.

'Huh?' Mikey noticed.

Wincing at the pain, Mikey bent down to pick it up. Holding it to his face, he instantly recognised the shape: it was an old key.

As he turned it left and right in front of his face, fragments of last night's half remembered dream floated back to him.

Mikey remembered the final words Benjamin had left him with.

To save yourself, you must hinder the girl's next ritual...

'Save myself?' Mikey wondered, 'is *this* the way I need to do it, by opening a door?'

Had that crazy old man left this for him?

Clutching the rusted key in his hand, Mikey knew that if there was one chance to end this nightmare for good, he needed to take it. Now, his apology to Amy would have to wait.

Limping, Mikey set off in the direction of Poppygrow House with the key clenched tightly in his grasp.

14

Chapter 13

Standing soaked at the doorstep of Poppygrow House, Mikey found himself face to face with Everlie.

"Oh," she sighed with an unimpressed glare, "it's you again, is it?"

The pressure of the bandage over her nose made her speech nasally. Mikey hated himself for doing that to her.

"Everlie," Mikey demanded as the afternoon storm battered him, "we need to talk."

"Be my guest," she laughed tiredly, motioning him inside, "it's your house too, isn't it?"

Turning her back to him, Everlie wandered through the hall, running her hands dreamily across the dust caked walls.

"So," she mused as she went, kicking Henry the hoover across the floor, "are we going to try and start over now or something?"

Standing in the hallway, Mikey just stared at her.

"What?" Everlie turned.

"Everlie," Mikey's voice was firm, "it's time for you to tell me the truth."

"What truth?"

"About the ritual."

Everlie gasped, collapsing against the wall.

"What ritual?" She panicked, holding her chest, "What the hell are you talking about?"

"Don't lie anymore," Mikey shook his head, coming closer, "you know exactly what I mean."

Everlie turned her head all around, but there was no one to help her, even Wicca remained out of sight.

"How did you find out about it?" She scowled at Mikey.

"Never mind that," he advanced, holding his arms out, "the question is what do *you* know about it?"

Everlie broke into a run before he could grab her, rushing around him towards the front door. Closer to it, Mikey kicked the door closed before she could reach it. With her exit blocked, Mikey trapped her against the closed exit.

"What does it matter to you anyway?" she bellowed at him, breathless.

Mikey lowered his forearm to Everlie's eye level. Everlie's eyes widened as she saw his wound, the bite was so much worse than it had been yesterday.

"It's got EVERYTHING to do with me!" Mikey raged, "I'm in danger, Everlie, and you're the only one who can help me!"

Everlie was unable to look away from the festering wounds on Mikey's arm.

"So, it's my fault yet again, huh?" she shuddered, her chin trembling, "it's always my fault."

Then, Everlie started to cry, mascara streaking down her face. Unsure, Mikey reached out to rest a hand on her shoulder.

"I'm so sorry Mikey," she interrupted him, swatting him away, "I had no idea I was hurting you."

"It's alright," he hushed, "but please, just explain to me what's happening around here. Please!"

Making him jump, she grabbed his hand. Mikey was forced to look down at her.

"I'll tell you everything," she asserted, wiping the stains off her round cheeks, "It all started when I was a teenager, when I met Maddy..."

*

"Maddy Pendragon was the girl next door. I was only 13 years old, Maddy was 18. At night, whenever I felt lonely in this little house, or if my parents were fighting, I used to look out of my window and watch her singing into her hairbrush and dancing around her pink bedroom," Everlie sighed wistfully, "it didn't take long for me to realise I had feelings for her."

Mikey choked on his coffee. Everlie stared at him over the rim of her mug on the chair opposite, sitting just as they had been when they'd first met.

"I hope *that's* not going to be an issue too," Everlie rolled her eyes, blowing the steam from her mug.

"What? No, no," Mikey gulped, his response triggered by something else, "carry on. Please."

Everlie's eyes glazed over with nostalgia, her shoulders loosening.

"Maddy was vibrant, energetic, carefree, and totally unlike me," Everlie smiled, shaking her head, "one day, totally out of the blue, she knocked on our front door and asked me to come out and play with her. It was the best. I wasn't lonely anymore."

Everlie fished out the heart shaped locket necklace from her top and rubbed it.

"She'll never know how much I needed her," Everlie sighed, staring at it, "even though she was so different, she was so much more experienced with life. And she helped me love myself."

There was a moment of silence, broken by a tearful sigh as Everlie continued.

"So, when my parents abandoned me, she stepped in so I wouldn't lose this house."

"Wait, hold up," Mikey interrupted, leaning forward, "how exactly did your parents 'abandon' you?"

"They just went away," Everlie shrugged.

"Went away?" Mikey pressed, leaning forward. "But how?"

"They died, okay?" she snapped.

"Okay but..." Mikey *needed* to know everything, "but *how*?"

"Stop!" Everlie threw her hands over her ears, "I don't want to talk about it!"

Mikey sank back into his chair. Opposite, Everlie was trembling, her lips pressed tightly together.

"All that matters is that it was my fault," Everlie hugged herself while looking up fearfully at the dingy walls of the house, "my parents hadn't planned to have me while living here. I was an accident."

Mikey didn't know what to say, so said nothing.

"By the end, my mother was so stressed that she fell ill, and my father..." Everlie was starting to struggle as her gaze dropped to the floor, "sometimes, I *honestly* thought that he truly cared about me, but one day I woke up and he was just... gone."

Mikey licked his dry lips.

"But that's when Maddy stepped in," Mikey guessed, "she became your legal guardian and you lived together, right?"

Everlie nodded, wiping her nose.

"This awful, dingy house somehow seemed so bright with her here," she sniffed, "There were still hard times for both of us from that day, of course. Maddy's parents were eventually put in a home, the pandemic happened, and the world just kept unravelling all around us every day, but Maddy... Maddy took charge of everything. She helped me get through it all. I don't think I'd still be here if it weren't for her."

Mikey nodded, remembering his own struggles across the last seven or so years. If only he'd known what his worst crisis would eventually be, he wouldn't have taken that time with Amy for granted.

"Maddy was the one who banned the internet in this house?" Mikey asked.

Everlie nodded.

"We took turns smashing the router with sticks out in the woods. Honestly, I think it was the best day of my life. She made me realise that the outside world could go completely to hell, but it didn't matter because we had each other," Everlie's smile was tinged with pain, "But then one day, everything changed."

Mikey wasn't sure he wanted to know but had to find out. The key in his pocket prickled him and the bite on his arm kept burning. He needed to focus on the *real* reason he was here.

"What happened?" he asked her, ears perked.

"I..." Everlie locked eyes with him, her stare deep and intense, "I confessed my feelings to Maddy. I told her that I loved her and... and that I wanted to be with her."

Mikey just nodded. Suddenly, Everlie grasped his hands.

"You have to understand," she pleaded, "there was only her in my life. I couldn't keep the way I felt inside any longer, I COULDN'T! I felt like I was going to explode."

"It's okay, Everlie, it's okay," Mikey hushed, listening intently, "but what happened next?"

"I don't know! Maddy just ran away," Everlie snapped, not angry at Mikey, but angry at life, "I screamed down the road for her to come back, but... but I never saw her again. In the morning, I found out she'd been killed."

Mikey watched her vacant expression as she relived the moment in her head, tears flowing silently. She faced him again, her streaking eyes seeking mercy and forgiveness.

"That's why you performed the ritual," Mikey looked her right in the eyes, "you wanted to use me as a conduit to talk to Maddy again."

"I wasn't ready to face this world alone," she confirmed, "I'm sorry I put you at risk Mikey. I'm so sorry..."

"It's fine," Mikey lied, "but how did you even learn about it?"

"Well," she shrugged, studying him, "how did *you* learn about it?"

Mikey was silent. He gulped, sweat dripping from his brow as the key pressed against his buttock. Everlie offered him a glib smirk.

"Maybe there are more people like us out there than we realise," she mused, shrugging.

The statement brought a chill to the air.

"I needed you, the new tenant of Maddy's room, to be the conduit for my ritual," Everlie sank back into her seat, seeming lighter from the confession, "I needed to speak to Maddy again, even if for nothing else than to tell her I was sorry for making her run away. I needed closure."

Everlie closed her eyes, spent.

"Everlie," Mikey approached, "we should try and perform the ritual for Maddy one last time, okay?"

Everlie surprised him by shaking her head.

"No," she stated simply.

"No?" Mikey tried to suppress his panic, "why not?"

"It's too dangerous," Everlie sighed, sinking deeper into the wicker chair, "Besides, I wasn't getting results anyway."

"What do you mean?"

"I heard *nothing* last night," she recalled, "But even when you were there, I could barely hear Maddy speaking through you on the other side of the door."

"But I saw her!" Mikey grabbed Everlie's hands, "she wants to talk to you too, Everlie!"

This made Everlie sit up in her chair, her head slanted curiously.

"Wait... you actually *saw* her?" Everlie asked, her eyes studying him, "you *saw* Maddy?"

"Yes!" Mikey nodded, leaning in, "the ritual was working, even if you didn't realise it!"

"But... all I could hear was a voice, *your* voice, whimpering through the door, telling me to 'stay away'," Everlie stated reproachfully.

Mikey gulped, the memory flaring up in his brain.

"I'm trying to protect her..."

'Remember why you're doing this,' a voice in Mikey's head resisted, 'do not fail!'

Strangely, the voice spoke in the same tone as creepy old Ben.

Mikey gripped Everlie harder, bringing her face closer to his.

"You must have misheard me," Mikey almost yanked her out of her seat, "Maddy wants a chance to say goodbye to you too, Everlie, to... to say sorry."

"Sorry?" Everlie shook her head, confused, "but what happened was my fault!"

"Everlie," Mikey patted her hand, "it's not too late to get your closure."

Everlie dropped back into the chair, wringing her hands.

"But what about *that*?" she noted, pointing at Mikey's bite mark.

Mikey checked his arm again. The throbbing of the wound seemed to let up with each lie that he told.

"I'll be fine," he faced her again, covering the mark with his hand, "With one last try, Maddy can speak through me. As the conduit, I can give you a chance, a real chance, to say goodbye."

Everlie dropped eye contact with him, looking at her hands.

"Is it worth it?" she asked out loud, "just to hear a passing whisper through a closed bedroom door?"

"It's better than nothing, right?"

Everlie cupped her reddening face in her hands, shaking.

"You're right," Everlie agreed, shaking her head, "If I don't get closure, I'll never be free."

Raising her head, they faced each other.

"I'm sure this will work, Everlie," Mikey assured her, nodding keenly, "I won't fail you. I promise."

*

The rest of the day went by in a flash. The two practical strangers, bonded only by trauma and a tenancy agreement, passed the time until gone midnight in silence punctuated by the odd toilet break and frequent turns to boil the kettle for further cups of tea.

At around three in the afternoon, Everlie left the living room for a toilet break. While she wasn't looking, Mikey used the opportunity to use her landline to make a telephone call. Watching the stairs through the bead curtain, Mikey dialled Amy's number. The tone rang and rang as Mikey watched for Everlie coming back down.

Ben's words from his half-remembered dream rang in his head.

"Everlie is a liar..."

If the old man had been telling the truth, Mikey needed a fail-safe. If everything failed, the only person who could possibly come to his rescue was Amy. Whether she would, however, was a different matter.

The phone rang. The receiver slipped inside Mikey's sweating palm.

"Hello, this is Amy Russell," a voice came through after he'd been holding the ringing phone for what felt like hours, "I can't come to the phone right now, please leave a message..."

The beep sounded. Mikey's heart hammered, more nervous about what he was going to say next than the ghost summoning ritual he was set to perform later this evening.

"Amy..." Mikey floundered, licking his dry lips, "I just want to say, I ..."

Then, Mikey heard the toilet flushing upstairs. The thumping of Everlie's big feet crossing the landing shook dust from the ceiling onto him.

"Listen, if I don't call you again after 2am tomorrow morning, something might have happened to me, okay?" Mikey hurried, not exactly sure what he was doing or why he was suddenly so afraid, "send help, I'll be at Poppygrow House. I... I'm sor..."

But the bead curtain peeled open to show Everlie standing there, watching him. He slammed the phone down before finishing.

"Who were you calling?" she asked.

"Oh, just my parents," Mikey twitched, scratching his chin, "just telling them I love them, you know?"

"Oh," Everlie swallowed, a note of sourness in her voice, "I see..."

They returned to their seats in the lounge and sat across in anxious silence for the rest of the day. Before long, it was 1.30am at night.

The single file trip up the familiar, rickety staircase was more like a funeral procession than what it should have been, a final chance for Everlie to be reunited with Maddy. Did either of them believe this would really work?

Did either of them have a choice?

Along the way, Everlie took a detour to her bedroom. Mikey's eyes followed her curiously as she emerged with a bundle of black candles under her arm.

"To help you relax?" Mikey asked.

"That, and the smell is nostalgic for me," Everlie told Mikey, laying them on the ground, "it helps me think of nice memories."

"Fair enough," Mikey nodded as he went in.

Mikey took in the familiar fixtures of his room, the ornate headboard, pink walls, and teddy bears were all as he'd left them. Home sweet home.

"Wait a minute," Everlie stopped him before he closed the door behind him, "I need to lock you in."

"Oh?" Mikey tried to sound like he didn't already know, "how come?"

"The closed door is not just a barrier, but a protective spiritual seal," Everlie explained as she ran her gloved hand down the side of the wood.

"Protection from what?"

"I'm not exactly sure."

"I see," Mikey mused, "so, is this info from a trusted source?"

"From my *only* source," Everlie shrugged, pulling a key out of the front of her black hoodie.

Mikey gulped dryly as he saw the key, aside from its freshly cut finish; it was an exact match for the rusted one currently nestled in his back pocket.

"Fair," Mikey tried to smile, locking eyes with Everlie as he closed the door behind him, "see you in about an hour I guess."

"See you," Everlie mouthed back at him and heaved the door shut.

Standing on the wooden flooring in the darkened room, Mikey heard the rattle of Everlie's key in the lock, followed by total silence. All he could hear was his own thumping heart.

For a reason he couldn't quite explain, Mikey went over to the bed and tucked himself under the covers. The bed was cold and unwelcoming.

"What am I doing here?" Mikey mumbled as he bunched the sheets up in his fists and pulled them to his face, like a toddler clutching his favourite blanket, "how did I get myself into this mess?"

'The story of my life,' Mikey thought.

Then, Maddy appeared before him.

CHAPTER 14

Mikey instantly remembered the sting of Maddy's dagger teeth digging into his arm and chest, so knew he needed to act fast. Whipping off the bed covers, Mikey landed on his feet and hastened across the darkened bedroom towards the door.

"Wait!" his pursuer called after him, extending a mitten-gloved hand, "what are you doing here?"

Mikey tried to ignore Maddy's spirit, pulling the rusted key from his pocket, and jamming it in the lock. One turn to the right, and this would all be over. So, why were his fingers trembling? Why couldn't he follow through?

Behind him, Maddy's icy breath came closer and closer.

"Why did you come *back* here?" Maddy wept, her voice growing coarser, more animal.

Mikey refused to turn around, refused to look at her. The metal handle in his fingers felt like 10 tons. The black wound on his arm pulsed angrily, spurring him on, while dark trails of blood were pulled backwards through the air by some unseen force.

"WHY DID YOU COME BACK HERE!?" Maddy screamed.

"I came back…" Mikey uttered, releasing the key, and holding himself up against the door, "because Everlie has something to say to you, Maddy."

The sound of Maddy's bare feet creaking along the floorboards suddenly ceased. Mikey turned around and faced her head on. The sight of her decaying face made him yelp. The spectre before him barely resembled a human anymore, let alone the vibrant, carefree blonde angel that Everlie had described. The bloody slit in Maddy's pink coat had grown into a gaping hole, and the muscles on her face had withered to the bone. She was rotting. The only parts of her that seemed alive were her eyes and mouth, hungry at the prospect of devouring the living morsel before her and barely holding back.

"The Dark will have full control of me soon," Maddy ducked her eyes away from him, "quick, say what you must!"

On the wall behind Maddy, a dark portal was forming, a hungry void filled with inky blackness and invisible, searching eyes. Mikey didn't have much time.

"Everlie is sorry, Maddy," he blurted, trying to mentally shut out the din of the emerging Dark, "she's sorry, okay?"

"Sorry?" Maddy's head slanted, the fierce features on her face slackening, "for what?"

Mikey steeled himself, looking into the gaunt spectre's oily black eyes.

"For what happened to you," Mikey stood up to her, "for making you run away that evening."

Maddy's nose twitched, curiously sniffing the air.

"She didn't make me run away," Maddy sniffed.

"Maddy…" Mikey stepped forward.

"I never wanted to be friends with Everlie!" Maddy suddenly roared, swinging her claws out at him as her eyes filled with angry tears, "at least, not at first."

Mikey stepped backwards, shocked.

"Wha..." he trembled, "*what?*"

Maddy turned her eyes to the floor, picking her blackened fingernails, wincing with pain as she recalled the bitter memories.

"When I was 18, I... I didn't *have* any friends my own age," Maddy's passionate speech was tinged with theatre, "everyone called me 'childish'."

Mikey stood in silence, remembering when Amy once called him the very same thing.

"I was a weirdo, a *freak,*" Maddy's speech swelled with anger and sadness, "I had no choice but to turn to that girl across the road, the one person who I knew was as lonely as me."

"But Everlie loved you Maddy," Mikey stepped towards her, "you meant the world to her!"

"I know that, and it made me feel better," Maddy cried, "But by the time I finally saw just how much she'd fallen for me, I... I couldn't face it."

"But then why buy a house with her?" Mikey struggled to understand, "why *live* with her?"

"Because I was a coward," Maddy hid her face from him, "I was just so desperate for love, and so scared of being alone..."

Maddy then looked up at him, her withered, rotting face wracked with pain.

"Please," she begged, "please at least just let me do this one thing right by Everlie, and please don't let the Dark get her."

Mikey was frozen in place, a deer in the headlights. Before him, Maddy's features started to twist and contort again, her nose turning to a snout and her teeth stretching out. Behind her, spreading across the wall like a stain on cloth, was the inky black well which was growing along the wall. The width of the otherworldly portal was now far wider than it had been last night, *far* wider, and the guttural chattering of lusty hunger from the lifeless void was now so intense that Mikey had to throw his hands over his ears.

"I... I'm not sure how much longer I can hold it back," Maddy snapped, her eyes blacker than ever, "if I talk to you any longer, the Dark will take us both!"

She grabbed both his arms.

"Please," Maddy gasped, "please just leave this place and never come back!"

Maddy's voice was now speaking in overlapping tongues, like another force was fighting for control of her body.

"Don't worry," Mikey assured her, shocked into motion, "I'll make sure of it!"

With that, Mikey charged towards the door, reaching out for the key Ben had left him. However, as he grabbed the handle, so did Maddy grab his arm and stop him. Mikey shrieked, her nails ripping through her glove and into his skin.

"Wait," Maddy cried, "what are you doing?"

"I'm ending this," Mikey gulped, sweating and bleeding, "I'm botching Everlie's ritual. I'm opening the door and breaking the seal."

Maddy's face clenched, not from the control of the Dark this time, but in an expression of very human panic.

"No. You *can't*!" Maddy almost screamed, "if the Dark meets the world of the living, it's like matter and antimatter colliding."

Mikey felt the blood swiftly drain from his face.

"What?" he trembled, struggling to fully understand.

"If it breaks free from this room, the Dark will consume everything," Maddy explained, now grasping his collar with both hands, "its hunger for life will devour this world!"

Mikey shook his head, not understanding. He tried to pull away, but Maddy wouldn't let him.

"But..." he trembled, "that old man told me that if I do this..."

Maddy's black eyes stared into him.

"*What* old man?" she screeched.

Mikey pulled away harder as Maddy's voice became one with the wailing dark void around her, not sure if the sound was even human anymore.

"He..." Mikey said with tears coming down his face, "he said his name was Benjamin..."

At the utterance of the name, Maddy's claws made Mikey wail as those nails ate into his flesh and he realised he'd made a terrible mistake. Maddy didn't say anything now, she just screamed.

'Focus,' the good part of his mind, a dying part, managed to call out to him in these final moments, 'FOCUS!'

Mikey was only able to take one last look at Maddy, her visage entirely corrupted. Her hungry eyes glowed at him. The black vortex behind her had now stretched across the whole of the bedroom wall, spilling out a wave of ghoulish shadows from its depths. Behind Maddy, the Dark swam through the air towards him, reaching out.

Mikey clenched his arms down at his sides, one arm in Maddy's grip, and one hand around the key in the door. He knew what he needed to do, and he released the key.

Mikey let the door remain shut, keeping the spiritual barrier closed. Inside his head, the voice of the Dark screamed in outrage. His bite wound burned in protest. Maddy's open mouth lunged forward, ready to drag Mikey away into her world of darkness.

"Amy," was Mikey's final conscious thought before shutting his eyes, "I'm so sorry…"

*

Moments later, Mikey opened his eyes. He was in Maddy Pendragon's bedroom. It was still dark, but the room was empty.

"What the?" Mikey gasped, collapsing in shock.

Holding himself up with two trembling, goose-pimpled arms on the wood slatted flooring, Mikey's gaze flitted around the empty room.

"What?" He asked in the silence, his head spinning, "What? What?"

The room was now silent. No dark void, no Maddy, no ravenous din of hungry entities from beyond this world. Mikey was now all alone. The baby pink walls had returned to normal, and the ripped-up bits of Taylor Swift poster leaned messily in the room's corner, right where he'd left them. The only eyes in the room were the black buttons of the teddy bears sitting atop the wardrobe and dressers.

The Dark was gone.

Mikey's hand flew up to his chest as he lay on his back. Gradually, he felt his panic melting away. His breathing returned to normal. Lying on his back, Mikey checked the bite mark on his arm. It was almost fully healed.

"I've done it!" Mikey gasped in the cold air, wiping a layer of sweat from his face, "I've *won!*"

But no, it can't have been him. It must have all been Everlie. From outside the room, she must have decided to prematurely end the ritual at just the right moment. She had saved him, Maddy, and maybe even the whole world.

"Everlie!" Mikey cried at the top of his lungs, not caring if any neighbours heard him at this hour, "I could KISS you!"

There was no reply from the other side of the door.

Never happier to still be in the world of the living, Mikey skipped over to the bedroom door and grabbed the key, flicking it to the right. Busting out into the landing, Mikey couldn't wait to see that strange goth girl's fat little face if she was still sitting outside.

But she wasn't.

The black candles were still burning, arranged in a neat semi-circle, but there was no one sitting in the middle of them. The door to Everlie's bedroom was wide open too, showing that no one was in there either.

"Everlie?" Mikey called out, scanning the landing, "where are you?"

Then, he heard a scream from downstairs.

16

Chapter 15

Three minutes earlier, Amy had been walking towards Poppygrow House, looking for Mikey. The sidewalks were empty, but that somehow didn't make her feel any safer. She pulled her cotton cardigan tighter around her bosom, the late summer evening felt like the dead of winter.

Something was going on in this town, something dangerous, and all Amy knew was that it somehow involved that place Mikey had moved into: Poppygrow House.

Prompted by the weird circumstances and inconsistencies in Mikey's story from back at the coffee shop, as well as the weird voice message he'd left earlier, Amy had spent the entire day investigating the history of that weird place. After browsing some local news articles, she'd discovered that Poppygrow had also been the home of that poor girl who was found brutally stabbed down by the river some weeks ago. Had Mikey been involved with that too? Amy didn't know for sure. All she knew was that, although Mikey was an idiot, he wasn't dangerous, and he certainly wasn't a killer. They'd been together long enough for her to know that much at least. Therefore, when his call hadn't come through at gone two in the morning, she felt he might be in danger.

'He was standing over you with a knife!' the rational part of Amy's brain screamed, 'are you *sure* he's not the dangerous one?'

"Yes," she huffed into the air as she carried on walking down the street, "whoever it was that tried to stab me, it wasn't really him. It can't have been."

Listening to herself, she knew it sounded mad, which was why she hadn't been able to say anything to the police (besides, she didn't want to implicate Mikey in any wrongdoing). She'd even tried calling him herself, but the silly bastard had left his phone at her place after she'd evicted him. Tonight, as she'd been lying awake, she felt she had no choice but to go and check the situation out for herself. Truthfully, she was worried. *Really* worried.

'Why do you care so much about what happens to Mikey anyway?' that rational part of her brain asked, 'Maybe it's better to let him go his own way!'

The offer was tempting. After all the little annoyances he'd put her through, like always forgetting to tidy up after himself, to the big annoyances like the argument which had caused their split in the first place, Amy couldn't help but imagine how much easier life might be without him. However, at the same time, there was also a part of her which blamed herself for their relationship failing. Maybe it was due to the pity she felt whenever her parents poured scorn on his 'under-achievements', or the fact that Amy was always ignoring how uncomfortable Mikey's troublesome habits, big or small, made her feel until it was too late.

A boy who was too impulsive and a girl who wasn't impulsive enough, maybe that's why they were a perfect fit.

'Shut up,' she finally scolded herself.

She was close to the house now. According to her phone, she just needed to cross the road at the park, and she'd be there. The black house seemed to blend in with the night, but the garish burgundy front door was hard to miss. Amy stalked up towards Poppygrow's entrance, her slow footsteps were the only sound around. Amy steeled herself as she prepared to knock on it.

But something was wrong. The front door was open.

Stepping up for a closer look, the darkened hallway invited her in. Even from the outside, she could see the place was an absolute pigsty.

"Hello?" she called into the black house, creeping up to the open door.

Silence.

The air became colder the closer she got. There were no signs of life inside.

But then, something rushed out. Amy pulled back, not quick enough to avoid the screaming creature that came barrelling out of the front door with its claws out. Amy let out a gasp as the furry creature went skittering between her legs out of the front door like a bat out of hell. Amy caught her breath as she watched the thing go.

"A cat?" she asked the night, putting a foot through the doorway.

Then, she heard another sound. It was Mikey, yelling something from upstairs. He sounded scared.

"Mikey?" she spun around, barrelling inside, "hang on Mikey, I'm coming!"

But as she ran in, she came face to face with a tall, gaunt stranger who was standing silently on the staircase. Amy doubled back, gripping the inner wall for support, and her hand skidded through the layer of dirt caked on it.

The figure on the stairs, half covered in shadow, was looking at her with wide staring eyes that glistened. The faint light through the door highlighted every crack and wrinkle on his naked body, fully exposed under his open coat. His expression was hidden by darkness, but Amy could immediately sense that he was hungry.

He released a low, lusty breath.

Amy spun on her heels, trying to run, but this man reached out and grabbed a fistful of her hair.

She screamed.

*

Moments before this, Benjamin Bonus had excitedly snatched the house key out of his coat pocket and stabbed it in the lock of Poppygrow House. He was finally coming home.

At that moment, everything was going as he'd planned. Or rather, as the Dark had planned. Clumsily leaving the door open behind him, too focussed on his mission, Ben wandered into the house with the flaps of his tattered coat swinging open. Benjamin drank in the memories as he climbed the stairs of his old home. The house had fallen into disrepair, a mere shadow of its former self thanks to his daughter's negligence, but it was still home to him.

Nattering in the back of his mind, like it often did, was the Dark. It had been against Ben coming back here in the final moments before its plan came to full fruition. However, Ben's will had been too strong. Besides, Ben had been doing the Dark's bidding for many years now, so hadn't he at least earned a chance to visit home just before the end?

After leaving the young man with the key, Ben had watched from a distance, making sure he did everything as Ben had instructed him. Mikey had performed admirably. Now, all that remained was for Mikey to break the seal and let the Dark spill forth into the world of the living. The Dark would have its fill at last.

Striding through the hallway of Poppygrow House, Ben followed the scent of the candles on the second floor. The ritual was clearly taking place, and Ben couldn't resist the temptation to take one last look at his daughter's face before the end. This was his moment. Whether she knew it or not, this was Everlie's moment too. Life was transitory, but the Dark would be eternal.

However, that's when he heard a small, angry snarling sound at his feet. Before he could look down, something was scratching his bare leg.

"Argh!" Ben winced, looking down.

The cat, Wicca, had sneaked up the steps and now stared up at the intruder with hate-filled eyes, its back arched and ready to pounce. Ben should have disposed of this wretched beast long ago.

"Shoo!" Ben hissed, kicking the cat in the face.

The force seemed to be enough, sending the creature skittering out of the open door and into the night. Ben sighed in relief. However, the cat's exit ushered a new arrival, a mousy yelp which arose from just outside the door. Someone was coming in.

'No,' Ben trembled, not wanting it to be true, 'go AWAY! You can't interrupt this moment!'

Before Ben could say or do anything, the interloper had wandered into the house behind him. Their gazes connected, and Ben recognised her immediately. He had seen this fair, dark-skinned creature sitting with Mikey in the coffee shop a few days ago. Clearly, she had come by to do some snooping, but Ben wouldn't stand for it, not now.

Turning on her heels, the woman tried to get away upon seeing him, but Ben wouldn't have it. As the Dark spurred him on with its rage and frustration, Ben reached out his bony fingers and grabbed her hair. However, the girl launched a backwards kick which connected with Ben's shin. Losing his balance on the step, Ben cried out, toppled over, and landed on his face.

'DO NOT LET HER ESCAPE!' the Dark wailed inside Ben's mind, "DO NOT LET HER RUIN THIS!'

'I won't!' he assured it, for the final time, 'I won't, I won't, I won't!'

*

Amy's adrenaline kicked into overdrive. She did a quick turn towards the half open red door and pulled it open, ready to dart into the night. However, she didn't see the rapid motion of Benjamin pulling out his blade. Lying on his face, her attacker held the one-armed scissor in the air.

"I WON'T!!" he screamed as he plunged it down into Amy's heel.

Amy gasped, falling over in the doorway, and was forced to take a sharp intake of breath as the frame connected with her ribcage, but the pain was hardly noticeable compared to the agony of her foot. Riding through the pain, she felt the horrible old man mounting her fallen body. Wriggling, Amy swung onto her side and clawed her attacker's face. It was no use; Amy knew from the terrible hunger in his eyes that he wasn't going to give up easily. Ben then raised his weapon to the sky, its sharp edge glistening in the moonlight.

Amy screamed again, not out of fear, but for help.

"Mikey!" was the only name she could think of, "MIKEY!"

The man plunged the scissors down.

*

'Oh no,' Ben realised, Amy's bleeding body beneath him, 'oh no, oh no, no no no!'

Her scream would surely have attracted attention.

'You've failed,' the Dark hissed inside his mind, 'you know what that means...'

"NO!"

Ben's hands went for his weapon. Facing the reality of another year, another day, another *second* with this horrible, scheming Dark trapped inside his brain and controlling him like a puppet, and punishing him with mental agony when he refused.

"NO! NO! NOOOO!" Ben screamed in a frenzy, straddling the fallen woman, "This was supposed to WORK!"

When Ben returned to his senses, he was still sitting on the woman. She was choking, bleeding. Looking down at her, Ben found that his body and beard were dripping with the girl's blood. The one-armed scissor was slick in his hand.

'Strange,' Ben thought as he stared down at her curiously, 'it's just like what happened when I last spoke with Maddy.'

"Dad?" a soft voice called from up the stairs behind him, "is that you?"

Ben turned around to see the face of his daughter, so much older now, staring down at him from the top of the stairwell. Ben smiled, happy to see her. At first, she just seemed confused, but when the light of the street outside highlighted the bloody mess of the girl he had mutilated lying in the doorway, she let out a scream.

"Everlie... it wasn't my fault..." Ben smiled through the tears on his bloody face, "we should never have messed with the Dark. We should never have tried to talk to Mum..."

Everlie remained silent, her face taut with fear and confusion.

Still sitting on the choking girl, Ben released a defeated sigh. Realising that he'd failed the Dark once again, and that it would not let him off easy this time, he held up the one-armed scissor. As quickly as he could before the Dark could stop him, he stabbed himself through the neck.

*

"DAD!!!"

Mikey rushed out of his room into the aftermath of a bloodbath. The first thing he saw was the half-naked body of Ben, the old creep from the underpass, lying slumped against the open front door with a gold handle jutting out of his neck.

"Fuck!" Mikey reeled, propping himself up against the wall.

Everlie, meanwhile, had collapsed onto her knees at the top of the stairs.

"What the fuck happened!?" Mikey went to her, not quite understanding what he was even witnessing out here.

Everlie didn't seem to notice him.

"Dad..." she just whimpered again with both hands over her mouth, "Dad... oh God no..."

At first, Mikey leant down to Everlie's level and put his arm around her.

"It's okay Everlie," Mikey tried to soothe, holding her tightly, "everything will be..."

But then Mikey saw the second body. The woman was propped up against the wall next to the door, coughing blood down her front. Mikey's whole body went numb.

"AMY!" Mikey shrieked.

Leaving Everlie's side, Mikey rushed down the stairs two at a time, practically falling over himself. Landing on the floor, he dragged his knees through the pooling blood towards where Amy was lying.

"I'm here Amy, I'm here," he hushed in her ear, knowing not to move her, "it's going to be okay babe, it's going to be okay!"

With the last of her strength, Amy rolled her eyes over to him, even managing to raise a little smile between rasping coughs.

"Mikey?" she struggled, her red-soaked mouth cocked in a relieved grin, "is that you?"

"I'm here Amy," Mikey found himself laughing as he stroked her dark hair, "I'm here for you babe."

Amy shut her eyes. She looked tranquil, but her strength was fading fast. Her skin was losing its colour, and her blood was pooling heavily against Mikey's legs.

"Stay with me Amy," Mikey begged, utterly convinced that his words would do the trick, "stay with me!"

"Mi... key..." Amy managed to break out of her seizure and cup her left arm around his neck, drawing him closer.

Her skin was so cold.

"I... I..."

"What is it, Amy?" Mikey clutched Amy's hands as tears fell down his face, "what is it?"

Choking on her own blood, Amy tried to finish her sentence but couldn't.

She now belonged to the Dark.

Epilogue

"Do you still want to do this?" Everlie asked him.

Staring at the floor, holding himself, Mikey nodded.

"I have no choice," Mikey replied, wiping away tears of determination, "I need to find out what Amy was trying to say to me."

Outside, a police siren went by, probably on its way to the murder site at Poppygrow House where the bodies of Benjamin Bonus and Amy Russell were still lying. Hiding in the living room of Amy's old house, Mikey wondered if Everlie knew, like he did, that the door to Amy's bedroom had no lock on it. Maybe she didn't care either.

They had waited for the hour of 2am the next day in stone cold silence. There was no need for words anyway. They both knew exactly what the other was thinking.

Mikey felt like death, and Everlie looked about the same. Only now did Mikey realise what this week's series of late-night antics had contributed to his mental and physical health.

'I'll have plenty of time to rest after all this,' he thought with a grim laugh, 'an eternity.'

Hidden under his t-shirt, the lingering wounds on Mikey's chest and arm started to throb excitedly at this thought.

"Showtime, I guess," Everlie suddenly announced as she heaved off the same sofa Mikey had been sleeping on just two nights earlier.

Mikey checked his phone. 2am. She was right. They went to Amy's room and Mikey waited on the outside of the door, keeping his best memories of Amy in his head.

"See you in about an hour, I guess?" Mikey muttered to Everlie just before she closed the door.

Everlie didn't even respond.

Sitting outside Amy's room, legs crossed, Mikey bowed his head and tried to make himself recall only the best memories of his time with Amy while sitting there in total darkness and silence...

...Their trip to York, the stir fry rice she made every Thursday, the way she used to laugh at his stupid jokes...

Mikey sat for about fifteen minutes, wringing his feelings dry, but nothing seemed to be happening. He realised he might never get the opportunity to say goodbye to her, to say sorry for being such a rotten boyfriend...

Then, he started to cry.

"Mikey?"

The little voice whispered from the other side of the door. Mikey sat up, pawing at the lacquered wood. It was Everlie's voice, but there was no disguising the dainty textures and tone beneath it. It was *her*.

"Amy!" Mikey cried, getting to his feet, "there's something I have to tell you!"

"Mikey, I'm scared," her whimpering voice came through, "what's going on? Where am I?"

The bedroom door handle started to turn.

"No!" Mikey clapped his hands on the door, trying to stop her, "Amy DON'T!"

But it was too late. Using Everlie's body as a conduit, Amy opened the bedroom door which separated them. Mikey shielded his face as a sonic boom exploded in his face, breaking the fragile seal between the world of the Dark and the world of the living.

"Mikey?" Amy's voice repeated.

Lowering his arms, Mikey looked deep into the eyes of the sad young woman in the black hoodie top, with fishnet sleeves going up her arms, staring back at him. Inside Everlie's pained, black rimmed eyes, Mikey saw Amy's gaze.

"Mikey?" Amy asked again, looking down at the body she didn't recognise, "what is this? what's happening to me?"

Behind her, Mikey saw a dark vortex growing across the wall. He didn't have much time.

"It's okay Amy, I just needed to tell you that I was wrong," Mikey told her, stepping forward and cupping Everlie's face in his hands, "And that I'm sorry. I'm so sorry."

"Mikey, I..." Amy stuttered, "I was trying to tell you that I forgive you."

"Oh, Amy..."

Mikey and Amy embraced. Behind them, the Dark rushed forth through the broken seal.

Within moments of Mikey's late admission, the Dark entered the realm of the living, swiftly spreading, devouring, until our world was rendered into a plane of eternal, lifeless dark.

The End

About the Author

L.W. Young graduated from the University of Kent with a BA Honors degree in English literature and creative writing. He has experience with writing for theater, film and YouTube, and is a passionate advocate of mindfulness and raising awareness of mental health issues. His favourite authors and influences include an eclectic bag: ranging from Stephen King to Cormac McCarthy to Ray chandler to David Mitchell to Kazuyo Ishigoda to Margaret Atwood and Colson Whitehead. However, if you ask him, he would probably tell you his favourite books are the Point Horror novels he read in his High School library as a teenager.

Printed in Great Britain
by Amazon